ABORTION ARCADE

Also by Cameron Pierce

Shark Hunting in Paradise Garden
Ass Goblins of Auschwitz
Lost in Cat Brain Land
The Pickled Apocalypse of Pancake Island

Abortion Arcade

Cameron Pierce

Eraserhead Press
Portland, OR

ERASERHEAD PRESS
205 NE BRYANT
PORTLAND, OR 97211

WWW.ERASERHEADPRESS.COM

ISBN: 1-936383-53-5

Copyright © 2011 by Cameron Pierce

Cover art copyright © 2011 by Hauke Vagt

All rights reserved. No part of this book may be reproduced or transmitted in any form or by any means, electronic or mechanical, including photocopying, recording, or by any information storage and retrieval system, without the written consent of the publisher, except where permitted by law.

Printed in the USA.

CONTENTS

No Children
6

The Roadkill Quarterback of Heavy Metal High
73

The Destroyed Room
120

NO
Children

Where I Am and How Close to Death

There is a light that never goes out. This light hangs in the wedding tower. Tomorrow, I will sleep there for the first and final time. Tomorrow, I am getting married.

I'll make love for the first time.

The morning after, the dead people will come. They'll cut off my head and steal my brain.

My wife, hopefully Pym, will become pregnant and give birth to a child who will never know its father, as I never knew mine.

To the dead people, male humans are only good for one child, then they are slaughtered and de-brained.

Naked, I crawl out of the dirt hole I sleep in. The hot fog eats at my flesh.

I'm damn hungry but take my time walking to the feeding troughs. Wedding season never brings anything good to eat for breakfast, only leftovers from the previous night's celebration.

In the distance, a tumbleweed blows against the gargantuan brick wall that closes in around us like a fist squeezing an eyeball.

Breakfast Heart

"Fill your belly, son," my mother smiles. She scoots aside so that I can kneel beside her at the trough. Her face is bloody.

She sucks the meat off the severed thumb of a man. I know the hand belonged to a man and not a woman because it is a young hand, a boy's hand. Zombies harvest males at a young age, never females, unless the female proves infertile or dies of suicide or some natural cause. That is because females are for making babies. From the time they are first married off, most females give birth to six or seven children, each with a different husband.

A man can fill a woman with his seed for one night and then he must die. The zombies cut off his head. The zombies want his brain.

The rest of his body? Human food.

Zombies are wasteful, inefficient farmers, but they know how to keep our gene pool diverse.

I squeeze between my mother and a ratty bitch who could very well be my wife come tomorrow.

Humans don't choose who humans marry.

I dig around inside the trough, looking for some choice bits. My mother grabs my wrist and forces something wet and soft into my hand.

A human heart.

She tilts her neck so that I can see the bite marks lining her jugular. "A bastard nearly ripped my throat out for taking this away. However, I promised myself as a little girl that no son of mine would ever go to his wedding night without the nourishment of a heart. Eat it now so that your seed may be strong tomorrow."

I am my mother's fifth child. She birthed four boys before me. They all went to their wedding nights before I came along, so I've never known the company of a brother.

"Thank you for your troubles, mother."

I bite into the heart, savoring the brackish gravy that gushes from the inner chamber.

As I chew, savage eyes fall greedily upon me. Everyone knows that in a few days I'll be in the trough. I meet each pair of eyes, wondering if any of these women will be my wife.

I return to my hole after breakfast.

I don't feel like talking to anyone.

What I Keep Hidden in the Dirt

I doze to stave off the hot air. Even though I'm naked and underground, the heat is overwhelming. I toss and turn, my sweat transforming the dirt floor to mud.

I'm awakened a short time later by the prodding of a shit-stained claw.

This can only be one person: Robbie, the goblin child.

"Please wake up, Grieves," he says, speaking with a grating lisp.

Robbie came from an old mother who died giving birth to him. My mother took him in at a young age, so he is sort of like a younger brother to me. The front of his oversized head is sloped and wart-covered. Two large twisted horns jut from his forehead. From the neck down, smaller horns cover his tainted, green skin. A permanent wheeze emanates from his nostrils. His breath stinks because he's got this nasty habit of eating his own shit. It's why his hands are stained.

"Wake up, Grieves. Please wake up."

"Get out of my hole, you shitting bastard."

"But your mother told me to wake you. The bridal lottery for Bill's wedding is about to begin. Your mother said you ought to be there, owing that your wedding is tomorrow."

"Get on going. I'll be there shortly," I say.

"Right, see you there!" Robbie turns around and scuttles out of my hole.

Certain I'm alone again, I uncover the little wooden box I keep buried in the floor. I remove the box and pull out the two withered papers within. One is a letter from Pym, the only letter anyone ever wrote to me. We were crushes as children. At the age of seven, she found blood between her legs and was promptly married off to Wolf, then the oldest man, all wrinkly and gray. Wolf nearly fucked her to death on their wedding night.

Pym had given the note to me right before her wedding. In it, she promised that when I grew bigger, big enough to marry, that we would be married and unlike all the others who come together for one night only to be lost to each other, we would never part.

The other thing I keep in my box is a drawing, more recent than the letter. I drew this picture of Pym a year ago at most. Pym is thin and frail like most of the girls, except she does not resemble a diseased rat. Pym looks angelic. White hair, white skin, white eyes, white teeth, white tongue. I want nothing more than to be her husband so I can peer between her legs and see up inside her. I bet she is full of clouds.

I bet she will be chosen as my wife tomorrow.

I will be her third husband. Some say that is the best one to be.

I return the letter and the picture to the wooden box and rebury the box in its hole, thinking I'll give the picture to Pym as a wedding present.

Pym, be my wife.

I scamper out of my hole and off to Bill's bridal lottery.

The Bridal Lottery of a Good Man

Bill is a good man. So good I almost consider him a friend. He acts kindly toward everyone, even Robbie. Unlike most of us, Bill was not born on the farm. He lived as a wild man, a free man, for many years. Until the zombies captured him and brought him here. Bill is educated about the outside world and many other things as well. Upon his arrival, he took on the role of teacher. He has taught young and old alike. We know many things thanks to Bill. He told us about this place called City, where humans live free to this day. Now it is time for Bill to get married. A good man, that Bill.

People crowd around the stage, which is situated in the exact center of our enclosed prison habitat, or farm. Surrounded by so many people squeezing close around me, I try to forget that we're imprisoned by brick walls a hundred feet high. I try to forget that all important things end in death. So much excitement but these bad thoughts squelch it.

The crowd parts to let the zombies through. Bill stands onstage by himself, looking dignified but solemn.

Like an army of drunken owls, the crowd chants: "Who will be his bride? Who? Who? Who will be his bride? Who? Who?"

The zombies shamble onto the stage, maggots swimming in the flesh that falls off their bloody bones.

The zombies dress in blue overalls and yellow boots. Some of them wear straw hats. Others are missing their faces, preventing them from wearing hats. Those faceless ones hold their eyeballs in their outstretched hands to guide them. It must be inconvenient going around like that.

NO CHILDREN

Bill looks sad standing among the zombies.

For most of us men, our wedding day is the happiest day of our lives, but not for Bill. Being a wild man before the farm, he has a different sense of things.

"Who will be his bride? Who? Who? Who will be his bride? Who? Who?" the crowd chants.

A zombie onstage raises a scythe. This is the sign for everyone to shut up, so everyone shuts up.

We drop to our knees.

A second wave of zombies sweeps forward from behind. They push through the crowd, grabbing at the females, feeling them up and down, seeking potential brides for Bill.

A few minutes later, six females are dragged to the stage. Some go willingly. After all, getting married and having a child is one of the only things you can do as a farm animal. It's a reprieve from the typical boredom and misery. Other women are dragged by their limbs or hair. Not every woman wants to get knocked up and cart around another life in a bloated belly. They know they cannot fight. Everyone's helpless in their own way, but they fight anyhow.

I look at Bill. Will I wear a frown when I stand up there tomorrow? I doubt it. With Pym as my chosen bride, I'll beam a golden smile and welcome her into my arms. I'll feel like the goddamn sun itself.

And then I notice Pym standing onstage. She's among the six candidates for bride.

The crowd picks up their chant again: "Who will be his bride? Who? Who?"

Please not Pym. Please. Please.

The Decision

The crowd goes quiet as the zombies inspect the six candidates one by one. Four look pretty much alike: skin tinged brown with filth, sunken eyes, greasy hair down past slumped shoulders, decrepit muscles twitching in arms and legs as thin as carrots, and bulbous sponges of coagulated blood and grime between their legs. Only Pym and one other girl stand out. Pym because she's beautiful. The other girl because she looks more like a giant bird than a human being.

The zombies pass over the four look-alikes rather quickly. They sprawl them on their backs and perform routine bridal checks, shoving fingers in all their holes and worse.

They slap the bird woman around a bit. I suppose she would arouse anger in anyone, living or dead.

I close my eyes when they lay Pym down on the stage. My gnarled fingernails dig ridges into my flesh. I feel my palms open up and start to bleed. I feel as if I'll throw up.

The crowd cheers, signifying that the zombies have selected a bride.

When I look up at the stage, Bill and Pym are embracing.

My face a flurry of tears, I flee the bridal lottery, feeling like my heart has been gashed wide open by a colossal pitchfork. Those stupid dead people had to go and offer my bride to Bill.

Running back to my hole, I shit myself out of sadness.

How wretched! How pitiful!

What the fuck!

I throw myself down into my hole and claw at the walls, hoping to bury myself alive.

Kill Bill

A little while later, Bill comes calling.

"Stay out of my fucking hole," I shout up to him. I'm exhausted from digging, although I hardly made any impact on the hard-packed walls.

"Let me come down. I want a word with you."

"Shouldn't you be off marrying what's-her-name? Preparing to cream her with your sausage?"

"Oh come on, don't say that. Let me come down. I'm still the same old Bill. Good, reliable Bill. You trust me, remember?"

"Fine."

Bill climbs down into my hole. We sit face to face. He flinches at the sight or smell of me, perhaps both, but he's too kind to say anything and feigns indifference. I stare at him with the cold eyes of a dead person.

"My life is ruined," I say.

"I'm sorry," he says. "Why do you feel that way?"

"You're not sorry. If you were sorry, you would refuse to marry her. You would kill yourself or let them kill you, whatever it took, to prevent the marriage."

"My life is over tomorrow anyway, so—"

"So end it a day early, you selfish prig."

"Me selfish? Consider your words, Grieves. You're telling me I'm supposed to sacrifice my life so that you can feel a little bit happier."

"Why should you get the angel? I'm the one who loves her. With my luck, I'll end up with that bird girl."

"Marriage has nothing to do with love in this prison camp. It does in the free world, it does in City, but here, marriage is an obligatory death sentence. One night of stranger-fucking and in the morning a man must march grinning to his grave. The zombies were once like you and me. They know the weaknesses and hungers that drive the living flesh. They exploit us on every front."

"I don't care who or what they exploit. All I want is Pym."

"If it makes you feel any better, your love for Pym is safe. Pym means nothing to me. I'll enjoy her body tonight, but to me she's no different than any of the candidates. And sure as I stand here, I'll impregnate her. If I don't, they'll harvest her for being infertile. I assure you, though, your love for her is safe. She may be my bride, but I do not love anything about her."

"For her sake, I wish that you did."

"And for yours, I wish that you didn't. Love is unnatural for cattle. Even if Pym was chosen as your bride, your heart would be broken when you learned that she did not reciprocate your feelings. Pym, like myself and all others in this place, is incapable of loving anyone."

"That's not true. I love her and she loves me. We have always loved one another. Since we were children."

"You are alone in your feelings."

I want to show him Pym's letter, which proves that I am not alone, but Pym and I have never spoken to anyone about our love, not since the thrashing we received from some fellow children years ago after they found us kissing.

"I must be off. Should I expect to see you there tonight?"

I spit in his face and turn on my side.

"Very well," he says. "It was good knowing you, Grieves. You're a good person, even if you sometimes act or feel to the contrary."

He climbs out of my hole.

Good man, that Bill.

The Farewell Crackup

I go to the wedding, if for no other reason than to soak up the sunbeams of Pym's smile one last time as I offer her the picture I drew.

Before I go, I put on my only pair of clothes, the ones I intended to save for my wedding. I want Pym to see me wearing something nice. And since she'll not be my wife, I no longer care if my clothes are dirty tomorrow.

Robbie dances circles around me as I come toward the wedding congregation. "Your mother was looking for you," he says. "She wants you to sit beside her at the wedding feast."

"Tell her I'm offering a gift to the bride and will meet up with her later."

"A gift? What is it? Can I see?"

"Go away, you retard!"

I find Bill and Pym sitting at the head of a table on which zombies are stacking headless corpses specially barbecued for the occasion. The couple looks as if they are going to be sick.

"Grieves!" Bill leaps from his chair when he sees me, visibly relieved to have a center of focus that isn't barbecued human.

Pym, however, ignores me.

"Congratulations to both of you," I say, then narrowing my gaze on Pym, "I have a present for the bride, if she's willing to accept."

"Why of course she'll accept. Won't you my dear?" Bill says.

Pym fixes a blank stare on him. "Just because we're getting married doesn't make me your dear."

"Duly noted," Bill nods.

"I'm sorry to interrupt. I won't trouble you any further. Have a charming evening," I say, the bitterness in my voice like splintered wood fileting bare flesh.

"What about the gift?" Pym says.

"Excuse me?"

"Unless my ears misheard, you said you had a gift for me. If it's mine, hand it over. The least I'm due for this lousy affair is a present, though from you I shouldn't expect much."

"Very well," I say, withdrawing the picture from my breast pocket, confused and heartbroken by her behavior. She's acting more like we're strangers than two people who have been in love for most of our lives.

I lay the paper in her palm, trembling in fear as she eyes the tattered, folded-up picture. She unfolds it carefully.

She laughs pleasantly as she holds the picture before her. Bill and I join in, dissolving the tension.

Pym likes my picture!

Without warning, she tears the picture in half, then into fourths, eights, and sixteenths. "What a dreadful little drawing," she says. "I'm ashamed that you saw me a fit subject for your unskilled hand. You are a creepy little man."

"Don't you remember, Pym? We intended to marry each other. I love you and you love me. We swore to never part. We swore to go away from here someday, to live a life beyond the cattle farm."

Pym scoffs and tilts her chin up, looking away from me.

"Go sit down now," Bill says, laying a hand on my shoulder. "You're getting worked up."

I slap his hand down and point a finger in his face. "I should kick your ass."

"You're out of line."

"Let's fucking fight, man. Come on."

"Get out of here before they take you away."

"I will punch you in the face. I will seriously punch you in the face if you threaten me again."

"That wasn't a threat. It was the truth."

I look at Pym. "Come on, are you really going to marry this guy?"

"Leave Pym alone. You're getting emotional. Nobody needs this."

"I will beat your ass if you say her name again. Don't talk to me about my emotions. You are not my friend. You are a motherfucker. You are a—"

Several zombies leap on me at once. They wrestle me to the ground and twist my arms behind my back.

"I warned you," Bill says, shaking his head sadly. "You shouldn't have caused a scene."

"I will fuck this farm to death," I tell him.

"I'm sure you will," he says.

The zombies lift me to my feet and cart me away.

Everyone stares at me as the three zombies drag me from the area.

They toss me into a cage and lock the door.

I'll never see Pym again.

Mother at My Cage

I rise and grab the bars when the zombies in their helicopters rise into a sky that is dark too early, flying over the towering brick wall that encloses us, back to wherever it is that dead people live.

I only tear my eyes from the sky and become aware of the rust now caked beneath my fingernails when Mother approaches my cage.

"Is the ceremony over?" I ask her.

"No, it's only beginning," she says.

"What are you doing missing it?"

"I should ask the same of you."

I lower my eyes, ashamed. I wonder if she watched them cart me off.

"Do you want to tell me what happened?" she says.

"You didn't see it?"

"No, I had not yet arrived," she says, shaking her head.

"It was nothing. I became hyperactive. That's all."

"That's all? I heard rumors of certain confessions."

I say nothing.

"You weren't confessing anything, were you?" she says.

"I told Pym I love her."

"Do you love her?"

"Yes. Pym and I have always loved each other."

"Always?"

"Since we were children."

She scrunches her eyebrows and a darkness clouds her eyes. "That must not be true," she says. "That must not be true at all."

"I think about Pym a lot. She's always on my mind. I've been really excited about my marriage date since it was arranged because I'd dreamed that Pym would be my bride, that she would redeem me and give me a happy death."

"A happy death, yes, that's something we're all after."

I lower my voice and say, "I drew a picture of her."

"Did you show it to her?"

"Yes."

"And she laughed in your face."

"And tore it up right in front of me. It was so humiliating. I've never felt so embarrassed in my life. Then words started flying out of my mouth. I must've sounded like a madman or a drunkard, so delirious."

My mother smiles and nods, "Yes, you are in love."

"Why are you smiling? It's not a good thing. My life is over now. I'm ruined."

"I loved your father. He's the only husband of mine I ever loved. We were lucky enough to be paired up. Prior to our wedding night, I often slept in his hole."

"You mean . . . love does exist on the farm?"

"Of course it exists."

"Bill said it doesn't. He said love was just what the dead people used against us."

"Bill is a good man, but he's also a teacher. Teachers will tell you the saddest things they know so that you won't be disappointed later on. It's their job. Just as it's Pym's job to be Bill's bride, and that means ignoring you."

"But she's *marrying* Bill. The day before *my* wedding. If she had any idea how bad this hurts me, she couldn't possibly marry him."

"If she really loves you, it's hurting her just as bad." She shrugs. "Anyway, Bill will be decapitated by morning and lying headless in the meal trough in a week. Don't be mad at Bill."

"Bill is a good man. One of the best. Wise."

"No, Bill is human like the rest of us. He's seen more of the world, but his brain is the same size and it will end up in the same place. In fact, you and him will probably be shelf buddies in some brain market."

"You're not sad that I'm dying the day after tomorrow?"

"Oh, heavens no. I'm happy that my littlest lamb is finally being delivered to the slaughter. This is a cruel situation we're born into. If I weren't such a coward, I would have killed myself after my eldest son was born. I hate this life. I hate myself for bringing more people into it. I feel like a mean old cunt sometimes, when I think back on the life I've lived, then I get sad when I realize none of it's my fault. I wish I had guts to do something bold. Maybe stick a knife in my pussy and cut a big hole. Oh, what a big hole already."

"Mother, please . . ."

"Anyway, the ceremony should be almost over and I don't want to miss the celebration. I still get a thrill watching the dead lock the bride and groom in the wedding tower. Do you have any last words for your love? I'll impart your final message to her if you have one."

"No," I say, "I have nothing."

"Very well then."

I curl into the corner of the cage, weeping now, as my mother walks away.

I shiver on the cold floor, alone while the farm celebrates the marriage of Bill and Pym.

The smell of charred flesh carries over. My stomach grumbles, longing for some barbecue.

It is nearly dawn when the party dies down.

Horn in the Keyhole

I awake early on account of the morning heat, the chopping roar of the zombies' helicopters, and also the mortifying fact that it is my wedding day.

I'm still locked in the tiny cage, still heartbroken.

When I see Robbie skipping toward me, I welcome the sight of the little retard with a happy cry.

"Sorry I didn't come sooner. I ate so much barbecue last night that I puked and passed out. I awoke bright and early to say goodbye to Bill. His head came off nice and clean. When I grow up and get married, I hope my decapitation is that neat."

"What about Pym?"

Robbie shrugs. "I haven't seen her."

"She wasn't present at Bill's decapitation?"

"No."

I am filled with a selfish glee by this fact. It's a shame that she couldn't be bothered to hang around after the wedding night to witness the slaughter of her husband.

"Want me to get you out of here?"

"It's locked and some zombie has the key. At least I hope one of them has the key."

"The lock is pretty big. Let me see if I can fit one of my horns in the keyhole."

"Go for it."

Robbie twists his head around so that his forehead presses against the bars of the cage. He sticks his tongue out in concentration, carefully aligning his little left horn with the keyhole. The horn slides into the hole. He wiggles back and forth, grinding his horn against the interior of the box-shaped lock.

A little click and the door swings open. I step out of

the cage, feeling free even though I have never been free.

I thank Robbie. He smiles and asks if I'm ready for the wedding. I shrug. The lock hangs from his left horn like an ugly piece of fruit.

Swallow Your Dreams and Say Goodbye

I retreat to my hole for a final moment by myself. Some people live aboveground in teetering shanties. Not me. I've lived inside this dark and crowded space my whole life. I enjoy living underground. It's a shame I have to leave my home behind to spend my last night on earth in the wedding tower.

I think about cleaning out my hole so that somebody else can move in when I'm gone, but the layer of filth covering everything has calcified into a gray husk, like the insides of a fossilized whale.

The only thing for me to take or leave behind is the box buried in the ground. The box containing Pym's letter and nothing else. I could give the box away or leave it to chance and time. Either possibility leaves me cold. There must be another way, something better.

Haha, of course.

I eat the letter, chewing off tiny pieces, breaking down the weathered paper with my spit. The letter tastes like dust and skin. And when my body is dumped in the trough and the cannibals pick me apart, they'll ingest the letter. Maybe that will muster some true love in them.

I replace the box in the floor. Some poor explorer will climb down here one day and discover it and for a moment dream of treasure. Won't they be disappointed. An old box full of nothing.

My jaw feels sore by the time I swallow the last of the letter.

"Goodbye, hole. You were a good home."

I leave the place behind, ready to face the most important day of my life, fighting with myself to silence the questions looming over me.

Who will be my wife?
Will I be scared or sad when the zombies come for me in the morning?
Do I want to die?
Silence!
A bell rings out, signifying breakfast time.

How to Begin a Wedding Day

They let the leftovers from last night's feast sit out all night. Flies swarm the spoiled remains of half-eaten carcasses. Maggots stained red by barbecue sauce noodle about in convulsive gyrations. They carry granules of meat in their tiny jaws.

I arrive early today. I sit down at an empty bench in front of a broken leg hung with meat so juicy it ripples in the breeze. After a lifetime of eating people, I stand firm in my taste: I hate eating people, except for hearts and legs. I enjoy leg meat. And barbecued leg meat is the best. They only barbecue our food for wedding feasts. It's supposed to promote fertility. All other times we eat each other raw.

The benches quickly fill up as people come out from their homes for breakfast. Most look hung over and sleep-deprived, their eyes ringed by dark circles, a stoop in their step, but without exception they'll be at it again tonight, pigging out on the flesh of old friends, drinking past oblivion, only to return tomorrow to do it all over again. This is the way of the wedding season.

My mother walks up holding Ronnie by the hand. The lock still hangs from his horn. They sit down, one on each side of me.

"Ready for your big day?" my mother says.

"My heart is set on tomorrow morning."

My mother scoffs. "There's no reason to be grim. All of my other sons got married like perfect gentlemen. Ronnie says he thinks of you as his brother. You should act properly. Set an example for the youth. For the future."

"For what future, mother?"

"Do you mind if I move into your hole?" Ronnie asks me. "When I grow up, I want to be just like you."

"*That* future," my mother says.

I rip off a too-large bite of thigh meat with my teeth, but it's full of maggots. I get up from the table and head for the wide-open fields. And yes, those are tears in my eyes.

The Games We Played

I remember playing in this field by the brick wall with Pym. We played here every day for years. We made up our own games. When we were learning to count, we counted bricks in the wall. All day long for several weeks, we counted bricks. If we forgot what number came next, we made up our own numbers.

We played another game that we called Cloud Castle, where we lay on our backs in the tall grass and looked up at the sky. We pretended to be sky dragons who lived on clouds. Some days, Pym and I pretended to live on a cloud together. Our cloud castle, we said. Other days, mostly when one of us was annoyed with the other or feeling staunchly independent, we pretended to live alone on separate clouds. I remember the first time we encountered a cloudless sky after inventing this game. *Does this mean we're dead?* I asked. *No*, Pym said, *It means we've fallen to earth.* She leaned over and kissed me on the cheek. We held hands in silence until the sun went down, shocked by the butterflies howling in our chests. *On earth, as it is in the great cloud castle.*

The Bridal Lottery of a Sad Man

I hurry back to the farm square when the helicopters fly overhead. I push through the crowd and climb onto the stage. People bow their heads at me in ceremonious fashion.

In the distance, zombies land helicopters in empty fields, sweeping up gusts of sizzling dirt.

The sea of sunburned sweaty human faces splits in half, forming an aisle for the dead to pass through.

The crowd picks up their chant: "Who will be his bride? Who? Who?"

They drop to their knees and sink waist-deep in dust.

"Praise be to marriage," somebody shouts.

After the last zombie climbs onstage, the second wave of zombies, the sorting wave, sweeps from behind. They push through the human crowd, grabbing at the females, feeling them up, seeking potential brides for me.

For me this time.

I turn my eyes down, unable to handle watching the process and feeling sick from the close range of the zombies. They're clustered all around me, breathing down my neck, smelling of fungus and rot.

A few minutes later, six females are dragged to the stage. Some go willingly. Other women are dragged by their limbs or hair.

A zombie grabs my head and forces me to look up and address my potential brides.

I fall to my knees.

My mother is among the six candidates.

The zombies grab me beneath the arms and lift me up. They loosen their hold and I collapse again. They pick me up and maintain their hold this time, forcing me to bear witness.

NO CHILDREN

"Who will be his bride? Who? Who?" the crowd chants.

"Wait, there must be some mistake!" I shout, but remain unheard.

Please not my mother. Please. Please.

The crowd goes quiet as the zombies inspect the six candidates one by one. Four look pretty much alike: skin tinged brown from filth, sunken eyes, greasy hair down past slumped shoulders, decrepit muscles twitching in arms and legs as thin as carrots, and bulbous sponges of coagulated blood and grime between their legs. Only my mother and one other girl stand out. My mother because she's so old. The other girl because she looks more like an emaciated pig than a human being.

The dead people pass over the four lookalikes rather quickly. They sprawl them on their backs and perform routine bridal checks, shoving fingers in their holes and the like.

They slap the pig woman around a bit. For a moment I think, *Yeah, slap the little pig bitch around. Kill her.* Then I stop myself and feel bad. That pig might be my bride.

The crowd cheers as my mother and I are pushed together by the zombies around us. We are forced to embrace in a fashion that can only mean one thing.

Someone in the crowd laughs, then the whole crowd joins in. Ronnie is in the front row. He's the only one who isn't laughing. I look away from him, ashamed. I force my eyes to look beyond the crowd. Their scorn is the least of the horror. I think I see Pym parting from the crowd, walking away, but I can't be sure it's her.

My face a flurry of tears, I tear away from my mother and dive off the stage. People in the crowd punch me as I push through them, struggling to escape.

How wretched! How pitiful!

What the fuck!

Sitting in a Field of Tall Dead Grass, Waiting for the Bad Thing to Come

"Is it right to marry your mother?" Ronnie asks.

"No, it isn't right. It's unspeakable. What did I do to deserve this?"

"And if it's your son . . . by your mother . . . that makes your son your brother. And your brother your son."

"Yes, Ronnie, yes it does."

"She's old too. This will be her last child, won't it? They'll take her brains soon as the baby is out, leaving the poor boy all alone. You don't have to worry, though. I'll care for him real good. I'll treat him special. As my brother and my son. Just like you would do. And if it's a girl, well, I'll take care of her too."

"That's kind of you. Now would you please mind fucking off. My life is almost up and I've got better things to do than make small talk with a retard."

Ronnie runs off.

I sigh, relieved.

I try to make a list of all the people I want to say goodbye to before the zombies lock my mother and I in the wedding tower tonight. I fail to come up with a single name. Bill is dead, Pym as good as dead, and my mother my bride.

What the fuck.

In childhood I never left Pym's side. Then after her first marriage, I spent all my time either hiding away in my hole dreaming about her, or else getting an education from Bill. It's easy to forget how alone you are when the days pass endless and you are unwanted. Now I wish to call it all back and do my whole life over, but it's too late.

I could hide if I wanted, but the farm is too small.

NO CHILDREN

They would find me before I even had a chance to starve, so when the wedding bells ring, I get up and make my way back to the farm center, wondering if I'm strong enough to endure the torment and humiliation I've been dealt.

First Tacos, Last Meal

The dead fill the trough with barbecued headless humans. They unload several barrels of fermented blood from their helicopters, then they fly off. A few zombies remain behind to make sure we're brought to the wedding tower after the ceremony, for the wedding tower remains locked at all times. Only the dead hold the key.

My mother and I sit at the head of the trough. A mustachioed man presents me with the traditional wedding plate of brain. According to custom, every man is offered a meal of brain on his wedding day. I've been given brain tacos. I've always wanted to eat a taco. I lick my lips and pick one of them up.

"Congratulations," the mustachioed man says, slapping me on the back and knocking the taco out of my hand.

"Thanks," I say, stifling my irritation as I try to remember who he is.

He says, "My wedding is tomorrow, so I thought, you know, maybe you could give me some pointers."

"Pointers on what?"

"Getting married."

"You should ask a female about that. I've never been married before."

I hope my mother will interrupt our conversation so I can eat my last meal in peace, but she's too busy chatting with the man sitting next to her.

The mustachioed man waves his hand, dismissing me cheerfully and blushing red in the cheeks. "Oh, I don't mean the *wedding* wedding. I mean after the wedding. The good part."

"The good part?"

"What you do, like, in the wedding tower."

NO CHILDREN

I look at him blank-faced. The man awaits my answer, twisting the corners of his mustache into hairy spirals.

"You mean sex," I say.

"Sure, whatever you want to call it."

A woman with lank, muddy blonde hair sidles up to us. "Oh hey, look at these fantastic tacos," she says.

"I was thinking the same thing," the mustachioed man says, squeezing the woman's shoulder.

The mustachioed man lifts my tray of brain tacos. He and the muddy blonde walk away together.

I've always wanted to eat a taco. Now I will never know what they taste like.

I suppose even on a death farm, there is someone worth stealing tacos for, even if those tacos are a sad man's last meal.

Ceremony

My mother and I follow the procession of cattle to the wedding tower, where the ceremony is set to take place.

The base of the wedding tower is lit by flaming torches. The torches flicker in the hot breeze. Up in the highest window, I see the faint glimmer of the light that never goes out.

A dead person stands against the wall of the wedding tower, which is the single permanent structure on the farm, built up against the outer wall.

The zombie's jaw hangs slack, barely connected by two rotting tendons. A big, tattered book is open in his hands.

Dead people believe that if they don't read out of this book at marriage ceremonies, the married couple will not produce a child with worthy brains. *Like reading to plants*, Bill once remarked. He never told me what he meant by that.

The people in the crowd press close together despite the sweltering heat of late afternoon. They look well-fed, bleary-eyed, and contented. They're waiting to see the happy couple off into the wedding tower before returning to feast and drink until dawn.

This is my sixteenth wedding season, my last.

The crowd pushes my mother and I forward, into an aisle that parts the crowd and leads up to the zombie with the book.

The aisle is lined with human skulls broken at the top.

My mother looks happy. She smiles and nods as she takes my arm and urges me forward.

My legs are jelly. I am shaking all over.

This is so wrong.

When we stop before the zombie with the book, he

NO CHILDREN

begins reading but the words are just a jumble of lisps and grunts. I cannot understand the words he is saying.

"Just repeat after me," my mother whispers.

I repeat the words she says even though they mean nothing to me. And when she grabs my head and draws my lips into hers, I don't fight back.

Her tongue is a cobweb in my mouth.

Locked in the Wedding Tower

A second zombie stumbles up the aisle. The book-reading zombie throws the book aside and grabs my mother, restraining her arms behind her back. The other zombie grabs me in the same manner.

I think of breaking free, running into the crowd, trying to climb over the wall. I would fail, no doubt, but wouldn't that be better than impregnating my own mother, better than suffering through the night only to be executed in the morning?

"Give us a child, give us a child," the crowd chants.

The zombie holding my mother's arm removes a metal key from within its dusty ribcage. The zombie shoves the key into the lock.

The heavy wooden door swings open, creaking on broken hinges.

The crowd leans forward as one big ugly creature, trying to catch a glimpse of the staircase.

Tears drip off my chin and I scream a final time, "I will fuck this farm to death."

I hope that Pym is around to hear my final outcry.

The zombie holding my arms pushes me forward.

I step into the wedding tower for the first time.

We climb the staircase awkwardly. I stumble over every step, unable to keep my balance because of the stranglehold the zombie has on me. My mother, who has been dragged up these stairs on numerous occasions, ascends with grace.

The zombie holding me finally grows impatient, grunts angrily, and throws me down. Unable to catch myself, I crash face-first on the sharp wedge of a stair. I feel my right cheek split wide open. I bite my tongue, severing the tip and maybe more.

The zombie drags me by the hair to the top of the wedding tower. I spit blood and teeth all the way up.

My mother is thrown down on the floor beside me. She takes my face in her hands, inspecting the gash that has destroyed my cheek.

We both flinch when the door slams. The lock grinds into place. We are trapped in the high chamber of the wedding tower.

When I leave this place, it will be for my execution.

My mother shoves the bleeding side of my face into her tattered dress. She strokes my hair as her dress soaks up blood.

There is a slight scuffling sound on the other side of the door. My mother must feel me tense up. She says, "Don't worry. They will not return tonight. They're only fighting over which of them must stay behind on the farm. The one who stays will perform the execution in the morning."

Soon the scuffle ends and we hear the loud echo of boots stomping down the staircase.

"Give us a child, give us a child," the crowd chants outside, but their voices are nothing more than a muffled drone.

"No children," I say, letting the world go black around me. "No children."

The words stick like mush on my ruined tongue.

The Scream is Not My Own

"Come on, son, it is time for us to make love."

My mother stands up and tries to pull me after her.

I sink down beneath the window sill and place my bleeding face between my knees.

"Get the fuck away from me," I say.

When I look up, my mother is writhing around on the bed. She begs me to please impregnate her. She throws the pillows to the floor, promising to throw herself out the window this instant if I persist in refusing to give her a child. She tries to stand up, apparently to plunge to her death, but her legs are tangled in the blanket from all the writhing. She throws her arms up as her body, wrapped in a blanket cocoon, drops to the floor with a padded thud.

"Fine, I give up," she says. "If you won't fuck me, then kill me."

She wiggles out of the blanket and tears from it a long strip of fabric.

"You can strangle me with this," she says.

I blink stupidly.

"What's it going to be?" she says, gesturing with the shred of blanket.

"What do you mean?"

"If you're not going to fuck me, you're going to kill me."

"Mother, I can't do either of those things."

She breaks down on the floor, crying. "Please, just kill me or give me a baby. I'm not afraid to die, but please, don't leave me at the mercy of the dead people. If you kill me now, at least I won't feel alone. I don't want to die alone."

I bite my wounded cheek by accident.

"Please," she begs.

I get up and take the fabric from her. I twist it into a noose.

"Do it right over here," she says. She rises and steps beneath a buzzing bulb hanging by a string from the ceiling. The light that never goes out is not that impressive. Tears have cleared pink circles around my mother's eyes. The rest of her face is grimy and brown with dried barbecue sauce.

She smiles. My mother is fairly good-looking. She is not beautiful, but her body is strong and toned and her face is kind and round. She would have made a good wife a long time ago.

"This is where your father embraced me. He kissed me on the mouth, swept me off my feet, and carried me to the wedding bed."

She gazes out the window. I stand behind her now, watching her sway back and forth gently, as if she is being held by someone

"You had better do it now," she says.

And I know right then that the saddest things in life are always just ahead. First I lost Pym. Now I will kill my mother. Then my mother will be dead, leaving me alone until my own life ends tomorrow. Yes, the saddest things are always just ahead.

Numbly, I draw the noose around her neck and tighten it. After a few seconds, her fingers dig into the knotted sheet. Her arms swing back, trying to reach me. I tighten my hold, gritting my teeth. She slumps forward onto the sill of the window with a clunk. Her knees buckle and she slides onto the floor.

I close my eyes and look out the window to avoid the sight of her corpse. I feel filthy and violated.

Torches flicker in the distance. The cattle are feasting and drinking. I can hear the faint hum of voices carried up on the breeze. Even up here, I smell the barbecue. I feel a stab of rage, wishing that I'd had the nerve to stop that mustachioed bastard from stealing my last meal.

There are no bars across this window.

Mother could have jumped. She could have taken her own life and spared me the guilt.

I look down and remember the trouble with jumping.

It's the cage beneath the tower window. Beneath the window, a cage made out of bones rises out of the earth. The cage yawns like a hungry mouth, ready to swallow anyone who jumps. The bone cage is structured so that nobody who jumps dies. The cage breaks their fall, saves them so the dead people can find them alive in the morning. The dead flay jumpers. I've seen it happen once or twice.

I cannot blame my mother for choosing not to be flayed alive.

I glance over at my mother and feel betrayed, angry, cheated out of some unknown pleasure, but I did the right thing.

She is dead now anyway. No retarded bastard child can be born. This will not hurt anyone.

I close my eyes and conjure up Pym's face, her smooth white skin, her little white tongue, her cool, bright eyes.

I open my eyes and close my mouth and bury my face in my hands.

The screaming continues when I close my mouth.

I lift my head and look toward the window, where the screams are coming from.

Pym is at the window, hanging from the ledge.

It's she who's screaming now.

The Great Breast Rescue

I rush over to Pym and pull her into the tower. We collapse on the floor together. She's covered in blood.

"How did you get up here? What's happened to you?" I ask her.

She is still screaming. I hold her tight, squeezing her as hard as I can.

I slap her face. She blinks blearily and draws a ragged breath.

"What are you doing here? How did you get here?" I ask.

"I came," she props herself up on one elbow, shaking her head a little, "I came to rescue you and your mother."

"What the fuck?"

"I came to rescue you and your mother."

"I know, but how?"

She begins to hyperventilate.

After a few minutes she calms down and tells me what she has done.

She has cut off her breasts and fashioned them into suction cups in order to climb up the wedding tower and rescue me. Just as she climbed up the wedding tower, I can use her suction cup breasts to climb down and then scale the big brick wall, to enter the outside world and be free once and for all.

"Take my breasts and flee the farm," she says. Her voice is very hoarse.

"What about you?"

"I'll bleed to death, or else they'll slaughter me in the morning. You can get far enough by then if you start now."

"Why would you do this to yourself?"

"I love you, Grieves."

"You love me? How can you say you love me when you're pregnant with Bill's child?"

"I'm not pregnant. Anyway, did you really think I was going to profess my love in front of every single person on this farm, all of the dead people?"

"You're not pregnant? Then how are you alive? Why didn't they slaughter you this morning?"

"I found this in the feeding trough a couple days ago." She lifts her dress to pull something from between her legs.

At first, only a tiny hand appears, dangling like a cock, then a second hand, and a blackened head. She proceeds to remove a shriveled fetus from between her legs.

"Don't worry, it's not mine," she says. "I found it in the troughs, dead. I put it aside so that if I happened to be chosen as a bride this wedding season, I could put this inside myself and not be found out right away. After Wolf and the other man, I couldn't handle the agony of taking another husband, not while you were alive, at least."

Pym's admittance of love brings me to tears. I reach out to draw her close to me, but she recoils.

"Why did you kill your mother?"

"She asked me to kill her, so I did."

"Grieves. You idiot."

"How was I supposed to know you were going to come to the rescue?"

Pym's face looks strained and tender. Pitying, almost. This is such a huge shift from the cruel disdain she showed me last night when I gave her my drawing.

"Anyway, there's no time. If we meet again, I hope we live a happy life together. Right now you must go, get as far from here by morning as possible. Take my breasts and save yourself."

"Why can't you come with me?"

"There are only two breasts. Hurry now."

"Wait." I rush over to the bed and pull off the bottom

NO CHILDREN

sheet. I go over to Pym and crouch down behind her. I fold the sheet in half, long ways, and tie it around her midsection.

"This won't stop the bleeding entirely, but it should help some," I say.

"Thank you," she says.

She takes my hands and pulls me close. I bury my face in the crook of her neck. She twists around, naked except for the sheet bandage. I'm in awe of her bravery. She scaled the wedding tower naked.

She spreads her legs.

I get down on my knees between her damp and hairy thighs.

I feel myself stiffen and take off my clothes.

I lie down on top of her. Her body is warm, her flesh is soft.

Sliding into Pym, I squeeze my eyes tighter and feel myself floating into the puffy white clouds I always dreamed were inside of her.

I pump faster and faster until I lose control and then I scream. I scream out of rage and pity and anguish and fear and sadness and horror and love, but most of all I scream out of hope. A hope that I am already dead. A hope that I was never alive. A hope that time will freeze and I'll live right here in this beautiful moment forever. A hope that before my execution, I will perform an impossible trick and redeem everything.

I thrust one last violent time and come deep inside of Pym.

I pull out. A sticky string of semen connects the tip of my penis to her crotch. Dampness trickles out from between her hairy thighs.

"I love you," she says.

"I love you too."

"But you must go."

I nod and reach for my pants.

After slipping into my clothes, I pick up her severed breasts off the floor. She helps me tie the nipples, which have been elongated to serve as straps, around my wrists.

"Keep the flat, meaty side moist," she says.

"Will you be safe here?"

"I'm still young. Even with you gone, the zombies will spare me so the child may be born."

"What do you mean?"

"You've impregnated me. I can feel it."

I catch a glance of my mother's corpse on the floor and get an idea that just might save us.

"Pym, we can cut off my mother's breasts and turn them into suction cups. We can escape the farm together."

I begin scouring the room for a sharp object to severe my mother's breasts.

"Wait," Pym says. "I'm afraid that isn't possible."

I turn to face her. "Why not? Don't you want to go with me?"

She smiles at me. There's blood on her teeth. Now blood dribbles out of her mouth. Now I understand.

"You're bleeding to death," I say.

Tears roll down her cheeks. She shakes her head insistently. "No, I'll be strong. I'll stay alive, Grieves. I want to have our baby. Please, believe me. I'll stay strong. Now go."

She coughs, spraying a strand of crimson spittle, which hangs there from her mouth.

Without hands to draw her close to me, I lean in and suck the spittle rope into my mouth, bringing our mouths together. While making love we did not touch lips. This is our first kiss since childhood. She embraces me. I gently squeeze her breasts as if they are still attached. Then the moment is over. She pushes me away and collapses. She's already too weak to stand. There's no way she'll survive until the zombies unlock the tower in the morning.

"I'm coming back with help," I tell her. "I promise you,

NO CHILDREN

Pym, stay alive for me and I'll return. I'll take you to our cloud castle in the sky. I promise we'll be happy."

She nods, her face distorted by tears and blood.

I climb out of the window and force myself not to steal a final glance at her. The sight of her in this state destroys me. And she did this, she sacrificed herself, for me.

My hands are suctioned to the sill and my legs dangle in midair.

It is easy to underestimate the terror heights may induce, until you find yourself high as the moon itself, without any wings or cloud magic to keep you aloft, only the breasts of your one true love, who is dying and possibly pregnant.

"I love you, Pym."

I realize, though, in peering back into the room, that I forgot to bid farewell to my mother.

"Oh, and I love you too mother. You were always kind."

Her corpse says nothing.

"Go now. You do not know what you'll find beyond the great wall," Pym says, her voice hardly a whisper.

"I'm coming back for you. We're going to make it through, Pym."

I close my eyes and begin the long descent. For the second time in as many days, I believe I'm seeing Pym for the final time, but I told Pym I would return with help, and by the great cloud castle in the sky, I will.

Escape Partner

Down from the window, I crouch at the tower's base to recover my strength and determine my next course of action. With no way of knowing what lies beyond the great wall in any direction, I realize that no planning is possible. I must scale the wall and hope to come out lucky.

I stand up, careful not to set my hands in the dirt, afraid to weaken the suction strength of Pym's breasts.

I start toward the great wall in a semi-crouching jog, but I don't get far before a voice calls from behind, "Hey, wait up!"

I turn and look up to the window of the tower, my heart lifted in anticipation of Pym's face. Has she removed my mother's breasts after all, and mustered strength to climb down and escape the farm with me?

The window is empty. Pym is not calling, nor evening watching over my escape.

I start off again, but someone tugs at my elbow. I spin around, sure that a zombie has seen me escape.

I see the outline of two little horns. I sigh, relieved. It is only Robbie.

"Robbie! What are you doing here?"

He wipes his shit-stained mouth, looking guilty. "I was just sitting in your hole by myself when a head popped down. It was Pym. When she saw me, she fled. So I followed her to see what she was up to. I watched her climb the tower. Looks like she saved you, huh?"

I nod. "I'm going over the wall."

"Where's Pym?" Robbie asks, cocking his flat, horned head.

"Only one of us could make it down. I'm coming back for her, though. She'll die before morning if I don't."

I grab his shit-covered forearm and yank him to his feet. He jogs along, matching my pace. "Where are you going to go when you get over the wall?"

"We're going to City, Robbie, and you're coming with me." I don't know why I decide to bring him. Maybe because I don't want to be alone. Maybe because I have no idea how I'm going to rescue Pym. Maybe because I may need someone to throw in the way of danger, or to eat if there's no food out there. Maybe because he's small and will be easy to bring along. Maybe I like the little retard after all.

"I don't know…"

"You want to die here?"

"Well, who will look after your child?"

"Pym, who is carrying my child, will die before morning if we do not find a way out of here." I'm not totally positive that she's pregnant, but that's beside the point at the moment.

"How are you going to climb up the wall?"

"I've got these. They're from Pym." I raise the breasts strapped to my hands.

"Oh."

"Come on, let's go."

As we jog through the rows of little shacks I imagine what things would have been like if Pym had been naturally chosen as my bride. It would have been tender, sweet, loving, probably. We would have consummated our lifelong love. And then I would be dead. At least now we can aim for the impossible.

A happy ending.

Survival.

I feel like a child.

I miss my mother.

I want to go back.

I want to hold Pym's bleeding body, kiss the bloody meat where her beautiful breasts had been.

I cannot let her down.

Minor Death

The farm is strangely deserted. Everyone must have passed out early from the feast. No one is wandering about and no fires are lit.

I must have spent more time in the tower than I thought.

I am kicking up dust, walking fast.

We jog along in silence for several minutes. Finally we reach the west wall. I decide that will be the best to climb because it's on the complete opposite side of the farm as the wedding tower. It will provide the most darkness for cover.

I cringe a little as I lift Robbie up onto my back. He smells strongly of shit, and his clumpy hands stick to my flesh as he clasps hold of my shoulders.

I fumble around with the suction cup breasts for a moment. They are soft and pliable. I wonder if they will hold our weight.

I tighten my grip and press the left breast against the wall. It holds. I swing my right arm upward. The second breast slaps against the wall and holds. I pull us up slowly, not slackening my arms for fear that I won't be able to drag us level to the breasts again.

My whole body shakes with the effort. Halfway up, a brick comes loose under my foot. It lands on a shack built against the wall. There is a loud clanking sound. For a second we hang motionless. "Oh no," Robbie says.

"Shut up," I snap.

If anyone is in the shack, they must be too drunk to get up and investigate.

I peel the left breast from the wall and swing it upward. We are leaving an obvious trail of bloody breast prints.

When we get to the top of the wall, my arms feel like putty. I can barely move them. They tremble at my sides because I cannot bend my elbows, but we still have to get down the other side.

"We're pretty high up," Robbie says, leaning over the edge. He is holding on to one of the small steel spikes that protrude from the top of the wall. Fortunately, so many of the spikes have fallen that there are flat spaces large enough to stand in.

We stand atop the great wall, feeling small beneath a night sky more vast and dark than any we have seen in our lives.

Ringing the farm like sunrays is a network of steel girders, canals of blood and soggy carcasses, wooden buckets whose rusty-toothed jaws betray to us their purpose: de-braining skulls. The decrepitude and disrepair of the slaughterhouse suggest grander days. The farm today must be a pale shadow in light of former glories. I feel sorry for what my recent ancestors must have endured.

Robbie exhales a gasp of horror. I turn to him but he's unaware of me, his uncomprehending eyes fixed on the area beyond the immediate ring of death.

I turn to see what he's seeing, and reiterate his noise.

Beyond, there are trees. People trees. Trees in the shape of people, or people as tall as trees.

"What are they?" Robbie says.

"Houses. The zombies live inside of them. Bill told me about these, although I never believed him."

I know this because the tree people, or people trees, crook their arms so their palms lay flat to support a helicopter. Their hands are helicopter bays.

"Are they alive?" Robbie asks.

Green lights illuminate the eyes of some houses like hazy, dilated pupils, but most eyes are empty, lightless.

Their flesh is most perplexing of all.

These houses are made of brains.

This means two things:

1) The dead may eat our brains, but sustenance is a secondary purpose.

2) We are being farmed by the dead so they may use our brains as building material.

I keel over and vomit. Robbie gets sick himself. We puke over the wall, onto the dead side.

We live our whole lives believing we're food. We eat people too (out of necessity, of course) and so somehow it seemed okay that one day we would end up as food ourselves. It's the natural cycle.

Being house material is not part of the natural cycle.

Underneath the sickness, I'm enraged.

If we'd grown up knowing the complete story of death, maybe we'd get used to it by the time our turn came around.

Seeing our bodies wasted like this, though, is such a shame. If they wanted to build houses out of us, why not use our bones as well? Surely bones are more useful than brains.

Robbie and I are doomed. The brain tree people houses extend to the farthest reaches of the dark horizon.

"We've got one option to save Pym," I tell him.

He rubs his tear-streaked eyes. "What's our option?"

"We steal a chopper and fly like hell."

In silent agreement, he climbs onto my back and we descend, marking the first successful escape from the farm ever.

Although we haven't escaped yet.

We've only climbed a wall, and climbing a wall seems small in comparison to the unimaginable terror awaiting us at the bottom.

"Come on, Robbie," I say, squishing the breasts against the wall.

With some help he clambers onto my back again and I lower us down.

I Wish There Was More Surfing Happening

I untie the nipple straps and press Pym's breasts against my chest. They stick, secure.

"The ground is hollow," Robbie says.

"No it's not, you retard. We landed on something." It is too dark to see so I feel around on the ground. It is smooth, cold, and uneven. It feels like metal. Robbie crouches a few feet away, his pale green skin glowing in the darkness. Then he lets out a choked gasp and vanishes.

"Robbie!" I call hoarsely. I scamper to the spot where he disappeared. The metal ground drops out from under me.

I am falling.

I land painfully on one leg. There is a resounding crack, probably a bone breaking. Pain shoots through my body, white hot and blinding.

Robbie lies beside me. "Are you okay, Grieves?" he rasps.

"Help me up. I think I broke my leg."

"There's a thing here."

"Don't touch it."

Of course, Robbie touches it.

A whirring hiss electrifies the air.

A single light clicks on. Fortunately, Robbie and I are alone. I breathe deeply, pull myself up against a wall, and test my leg. Blinding pain. I collapse.

Faint stars are visible through the numerous holes in the ceiling. We must have fallen through a hole in the darkness.

I look over at Robbie. He is drenched in blood.

"Where are we?" he asks.

I gesture toward a huge vat of brains.

I manage to limp over to it. Maybe my leg isn't broken after all, but it hurts like shit.

Some of the brains have disintegrated. Others look fresh. They are all a reddish-gray and marinating in blood. Robbie must have landed in a spilled puddle of that blood.

Past the vat, there is a giant wooden hand.

Robbie walks over to it. A trail of little red footprints follows him.

"Robbie, come over here." I pull a pair of yellow boots and overalls from a cabinet on the wall. I slip the overalls over my tattered clothes. Robbie takes a pair of boots and overalls for himself.

I pull down another pair of overalls from the cabinet, return to the brain vat, and pile the freshest-looking brains into the overalls, then fold them up to form a sack.

"What are you doing?"

"We might need food during our escape. After we rescue Pym and make our escape, we might not come across food for a long time."

"What if the brains turn into houses in our stomachs?"

"You retard," I say, but I'm cut off because a zombie grabs me from behind.

Taken by surprise, I throw Robbie at the shambling dead person.

Robbie shrieks and lowers his head in fear. Rotten fangs bared, the zombie grabs for Robbie's skull, but Robbie charges with his little horns, knocking the dead person down.

Robbie stomps on the zombie's skull until his foot is just splashing around in a puddle of blood, brain juice, teeth, and broken skull.

I learn two things from this encounter. When zombies attack, throw Robbie at them. Also, never piss Robbie off. That means never calling him a retard again, if I can resist.

We look around, expecting more dead people, but everything is quiet and deserted.

"Maybe he was working late," I say.

"Maybe."

We proceed through the inner circle, puzzling over each new strange device.

"What do you think this one is for?" Robbie asks, gesturing toward a colossal upright rock slab engraved with symbols. "Do they flatten people under it?"

"No, I don't think this is meant to flatten people. The engravings must mean something. It could be a code of the dead."

"A code?"

"Rules to live by."

"The dead live by rules?"

I nod my head.

"Does that mean they're alive like you and me?"

"Well, they're industrious enough to farm and smart enough to utilize written language. I would say they're a lot like you and me."

Bad Brains

Robbie is banging around in the shadows ahead. I try to keep my weight off my bad leg, but every step is murder. I wonder if I should stop and try to set it, make a splint or a cast out of brains, but we need to keep moving. Who knows when all these wooden hands will come alive.

We have entered a section of the underground where the walls are lined with glass troughs. The troughs hold brains in various stages of growth. Some of the brains are shaped like people.

Robbie gags. He spits out a mouthful of brain.

"What's wrong?" I ask.

"These brains you grabbed are bad," he says, leaning against an empty trough covered in white dust. He drops melty, pulsing brain goop in my hand. I lick a little from my palm.

I spit it out. The brain tastes earthy and sour, like the decay that grows in the nooks and crannies of the body.

These brains are past the edible point. I try to wipe the taste off my tongue and look disgustedly at the overalls bulging with brains.

"Don't the dead people eat these?" Robbie asks, dropping the makeshift brain sack and wiping his bloody hand on the leg of his own too-large overalls.

"There must be a difference between house quality brains and edible ones. These brains were obviously meant to be turned into houses."

"Yeah, well they're nasty."

"And you eat your own shit."

We move along.

The ground is a little lighter now that gray light is seeping in through the holes in the ceiling. It is almost dawn.

NO CHILDREN

The brain pods and wooden hands appear older, greasier, and more rusted as we move along. A hairy layer of dust coats everything.

Robbie halts several feet in front of me, gazing straight up. I follow his gaze. He is peering through a hole in the ceiling. Through the hole, the head of an enormous zombie house can be seen: luminescent eyes and a gaping, glowing mouth. It is looking straight at us.

We stare up at the zombie house for a little while. The sky framing it is bluish brown.

"Look," Robbie whispers, pointing.

A wooden arm stretches out before us. It holds several lumpy objects.

In its palm, a human brain quivers and convulses. Bundles of red and blue cords flutter from the brainstem like tentacles. It is a half-formed circulatory system. The cord bundles are huge, huge enough to form the veins and arteries of a massive zombie.

"Is it alive?" Robbie is looking up at the zombie house again.

It hasn't moved. "No," I say, hoping I'm right. "Let's move on."

I shudder, imagining them rewiring my brain, growing it into a lifeless, gigantic replica of myself. And there's no way my bad brain is fit for consumption.

A Forest of People

We search for an exit, trying to keep out of direct view of the holes in the ceiling, afraid to be seen by the zombie houses even though they might not be alive.

The factory looks desolate, as if few workers have been here in years, and yet brains are everywhere. There are brains splattered on the floor, impaled on hooks, and even brains dried to the ceiling, as if someone threw them up there and they never came down.

Finally, we discover a gap in the wall large enough to crawl through. I shove Robbie through first. The sky is pinkish now. The zombies will be opening the wedding chamber soon. They will find two dead women and no man to harvest.

Maybe they will choose some random person from the crowd to harvest instead.

I hope it's that mustachioed bastard.

Outside the slaughterhouse, we're surrounded by giant zombies. I can no longer see the brick wall, only giant zombies in every direction.

Something sticky touches my hand and I jerk away.

It is only Robbie, reaching for me. I let him hold one finger as we look up at the giant zombies.

Every giant is rooted to the ground by mushy brain feet. Between the feet of the nearest zombie rises a spiral staircase, leading up into a little fissure between the legs. There are some windows in the torso, scattered haphazardly across the back of the structure. The arms of each zombie are stretched out similarly, forming a thin canopy above us. The heads are massive, some with huge black holes for eyes, some yellow circles in the distance. These zombies are taller than the wedding tower, but not as high

NO CHILDREN

as the brick wall, which explains why we could not see them from the farm. Their hands are helicopter pads.

I wonder if everything I'm seeing is true, or if what I know of the world is entirely wrong and zombies do not live inside of giant zombies, but everything I think and see and feel tells me that yes, zombies do live inside of giant zombies.

It makes me so sick.

I wonder if anyone on the farm knows where brains truly go once they are harvested.

As we stand frozen with our backs to the brain factory, a faint whirring echoes off the giant zombies. I recognize it soon enough as the sound of a helicopter.

I know what we have to do.

All my life, I have felt that everything is doomed, but Pym has always given me a little bit of hope. Now she is far from me, bleeding to death alone. Was the hope she instilled in me a monstrous illusion? Is she herself a monstrous illusion?

Would I persist in the fight for beauty, knowing that she was?

Yes.

Would I steal a helicopter for her?

Yes.

Would I give up my life?

Yes.

"Pym needs us," I say, as a helicopter bursts into sight from above.

Forced Entry

The giant zombies quiver in the pink and yellow light of dawn. Standing near the foot of one, I feel like a dwarf. I'm the size of the giant's big toe. The zombies crowd together, forming a gray canopy of limbs and torsos and heads that block out the light as we proceed out of the slaughterhouse. Between the legs of each giant, a spiral staircase rises, disappearing into a black chasm that appears to give entrance into the zombie house. The staircase in the wedding tower is identical, only much tinier.

Hopefully some passage from the groin leads to the helicopter landing hands.

I yank my finger from Robbie's grasp and limp quickly, seeking cover.

I nod my head toward the nearest ladder, letting Robbie know that's the one we're going to climb.

When I hit the stairs, my bad leg collapses under me. Robbie throws one arm across my shoulders and helps me to my feet.

Halfway up, the helicopter zooms in on us, hovering at close range. Flaming orbs erupt from tubes on both sides of the cockpit. The flames melt the lower half of the staircase into bubbling black goop.

They blast another round of the flaming orbs but miss us entirely, instead destroying the staircase of the giant zombie closest to the one we're climbing.

When we reach the top, a door made out of brains slides open and we clamber into the giant zombie, hopefully safe.

We proceed cautiously. The squishy floor muffles our footsteps.

A light switches on somewhere above us. The groan of

zombies breaks out in other corridors. The groaning nears.

I look around, searching for a way out, a place to hide, anything. Our only option is to return back through the door. We barely evaded the helicopter's attack the first time. I don't want to chance another round, but then hands break out of the walls around us.

Zombies are climbing out of the walls!

We flee through the door, ducking to avoid the chopper blades spinning perilously close to the entrance.

Backed against the outer wall, I stab a finger into the giant zombie's flesh. The surface breaks and my finger slides in. I pull my finger out. It is covered in brain goo.

"Hold your breath. We're going in," I say.

Robbie nods his head.

I throw my arms around him and dive into the inner thigh of the giant zombie.

We break through, and we swim like hell.

Climbing Again

We pop out in the middle of the giant zombie's back. That's as long as either of us could hold our breath, hopefully enough to throw our pursuers off course.

We dig our way up the backside, leaving behind a trail of gashes that heal over almost as soon as we make them.

I reach out to pull myself onto the shoulder. Now I can see the blades of a helicopter perched on the palm.

Then angry dead faces and clawed hands burst out of the brainy surface around me. The zombies have swum up and cut off our path.

I scramble onto the shoulder, kicking my feet into the folds of teeth and claws as Robbie does the same.

The zombies shout at me, but I cannot understand what they are saying. I'm not even sure if I'm meant to understand. Two hands clutch my bad leg and squeeze, breaking it if it wasn't already broken. I cry out.

More hands grab me, dragging me into the zombie house.

I flail my arms, hoping Robbie will help, but he's sinking as well, being dragged down. I wonder if we'll drown before they eat us, or if our brains will be turned into houses.

Then there is a creaking and a huge hand sweeps toward us from above. Another giant zombie bends forward, its eyes glowing yellow and its head so close and big that it smothers the brightening sky.

The hand plucks Robbie and me from the hands of the zombies pulling us under. It sets us right next to the helicopter on the palm of the giant we've been climbing.

The house has saved us.

I wonder if all houses are friendly, or if I happened to know the owner of this one's brain from the farm. *Are you*

NO CHILDREN

my father . . . my brother . . . Bill? I wonder.

    And then the head of the friendly giant is engulfed in flames.

Helicopter

The house we're on begins to move, leaning forward like it has a stomachache. All the houses near us start moving too, stretching out various limbs, trying to reach us, making obvious efforts to uproot their mushy feet and step to the aid of their fellow zombie house. Hopefully they don't blame us for its destruction.

More fiery blasts tear apart other zombie houses.

"Get in the helicopter!" I shout.

I leap into the machine and look around.

I have no idea how to fly a helicopter.

I feel intense sensations of anxiety coupled with crippling fear and physical panic.

Four massive fingers curl up in front of us. The giant we're on is closing its hand. Maybe this one is not a friend.

We are about to be crushed.

Robbie slaps something in front of me and the helicopter rises.

He has pressed a big green button marked GO.

I nod, feeling good about his decision. That was a good decision. GO is a good bet.

Four red arrows, one pointing up, one down, one left, and one right, encircle the GO button.

Feeling like maybe I know what those arrows mean, I punch up. And then left. The helicopter jerks in the directions indicated.

The helicopter shoots into the air.

Below us, the giant hand closes into a gelatinous fist.

Major Death

Fire swirls around us. We manage to steer clear of the direct blasts. We rise higher until the brick wall appears. It looks so small from up here. Strange to think that until today, it was my lifelong jailer. We zoom full-speed toward it.

I hope Pym has not already bled to death.

The zombie forest ends several hundred yards away from the tremendous brick wall. We are high enough up that we clear the wall as if it were nothing more than a dirt clod beneath our bare feet. The ground below looks gray and blotchy. I realize the blotches are a crowd of people gathered around the wedding tower.

A fireball whizzes by and explodes in the air over the wedding tower, followed by a second and a third.

"Robbie, try to see behind us. What's on our tail?"

"Helicopters," he says. "Everywhere."

I hook around the wedding tower, glimpsing a pale face in the window.

Pym.

She's not dead!

"Robbie, find the rope ladder like the ones the zombies use. When we fly close enough, throw the ladder out to Pym."

Fire bombs whiz past. The crowd around the wedding tower flees. Those people were waiting to witness my execution.

Helicopters swarm us. I can make out the faces of the dead people in the other helicopters. Hopefully their closeness will prevent others from firing on us. I don't know how zombies feel about killing their own kind.

Robbie prepares to throw the ladder.

Unsure how to get the helicopter to stop right outside the window of the tower without crashing on the bone cage, I press a whole bunch of buttons at once and scream,

"Throw it now!"

Robbie throws the ladder.

Pym dives out of the window. She cranes her arms for the ladder, careening into the jaws of the cage, looking like a fallen cloud creature. A ghost.

Her hands touch the ladder.

She stops falling.

She climbs.

Before she makes it into the helicopter, another ladder swings toward her. A zombie hangs from the end of the ladder.

Pym's mouth opens in a scream that is silenced by the helicopter's deafening roar.

The zombie swings level to her.

Climb, Pym, climb. It's not over yet.

The zombie punches her in the face. Her left hand loses grip of the ladder. The zombie reaches for her right hand as she struggles to regain her balance. If only she were stable, I could lift the helicopter and pull her up. Now it's too late.

Robbie grabs my hand and squeezes tightly. He smiles and drops my hand. I want to ask him what the fuck he thinks he's doing, but he jumps out of the helicopter before I get the chance.

Robbie plummets with his arms outspread like wings. He crashes into the zombie attacking Pym. The undead aggressor tries to hold on but falls after Robbie, leaving two rotted arms clutching the ladder.

Robbie and the armless zombie explode in a shower of blood on impact.

I'm staring at the mess they've left behind when Pym pulls herself into the helicopter. I smile at her and set the helicopter into motion.

My bad leg feels like it's burning to ash on the inside.

Will she bleed to death?

Followed by countless dead in their flying machines, we head east toward the risen sun.

Rise of the Tree People

The zombies in their helicopters close in around us, blasting fireballs and diminishing our survival rate by the second. We clear the great wall. If we die now, at least Pym and I will die together in the free world. The flames dance under us like a field of grass in summer. The gigantic zombies loom ahead and above. I press some dials on the control panel and the helicopter veers upward in a vertical ascent. We'll never make it. The people houses are too tall. I grab Pym's left hand and close my eyes, bracing myself to explode in a rain of fire and blood. "I love you," I shout, but my voice is sucked from my mouth by the din of the helicopters.

I remember a lesson about death that Bill once taught. "Dying feels good, studies report," he said. When someone said they knew firsthand that dying hurt, Bill shook his head and sighed and said, "It feels good because we fear it so damn much, and then we learn in our last gasp that it's easy. It's getting there that's hard and scary. That hard and scary part is only life."

I open my eyes to a scratchy wetness against my cheek.

Pym is licking my face. I look at her questioningly. She smiles, shrugs. Seeing her smile, I no longer feel scared. I smile back at her. I guess it must be easier to get through all the hard and scary parts that make up a life if you have someone to share them with. The zombies regulated our mating habits not only to produce the best genetic crop, but to alienate us from our essential nature, the throbbing, aching muscle that stirs our blood into a frenzied howling panic. When you have no one to turn to, no one to play games with, then you're no better than the undead. We are all so much worse alone, and aren't we always alone? Not me anymore. I'm in love.

Pym's wounds appear to have healed. The bleeding has stopped, at least. I don't want to ask her how it happened. Prodding this miracle might ruin the magic.

The zombie giants are moving now. They swing their massive hands in our direction, blocking out the sun and pitching the bright morning into darkness. I think they are going to crush us or slap us out of the sky, but their hands go on flying by, swirling up gusts of wind that rock our helicopter off its course.

We careen end over end as gargantuan hands and faces pass by. In the fragmentary rearview glimpses I get as we flip, I see that the zombie houses are uprooting themselves entirely from the ground. They swim together as a mass bigger than the sky, and they prevent the pursuing helicopters from passing. Maybe the giants retained some memory of when they were human. Whatever the reason, they have saved us.

Beefheart City

The zombie trees are thinning now. In the distance, tall dark forms jut out from the horizon like so many wedding towers.

"Do you think there are more giants?" Pym says. Now that the army of helicopters has fallen far behind us, we can speak and hear each other.

"No," I say.

We're so rattled there isn't anything more to say, until the zombie trees vanish entirely from the ground beneath us. We're flying over a flat gray field. The dark forms we saw in the distance rise taller in our view, rising high as the zombie trees. The dark forms do not look alive. They look like the wedding tower, only sadder and taller. These buildings are thin, wavering rusty things with broken windows. Crashed helicopters and other broken machines lie in decaying heaps on the ground like the scars of a broken face.

A yellow circle crossed over by straight yellow lines is painted on the top of each tall building. I recognize these as helicopter landing pads from the identical markings on the hands of the giants.

I press a few buttons and take the helicopter in for a landing. My guts settle back into their proper place as the helicopter slows down and descends. Flying must be disastrous for a person's health.

After we land, Pym and I sit still in the helicopter for a minute, silent and shocked that we have walked out on our old life, but we are here. We are alive.

We crawl out through the same side, hand in hand, afraid to part from each other for even a second. We walk to the edge of the building and look out on a dead skyline. We can see for miles, and in those miles we see nothing move.

"This must be City," Pym says.

I pull her away from the edge, feeling cold and vaguely disappointed. She's right. This must be City, but where are the people? Where is the civilization Bill spoke so much about? All gone. Dead, I suppose.

Pym and I walk to the other side of the rooftop, where an open doorway leads into the building like a tight black mouth.

We walk down some stairs until we come to a red door. We open the red door, which leads down some more dark stairs, which lead to another red door, which leads to more dark stairs, which lead to another red door, which leads to more dark stairs, which leads to a white door that looks as if it is made of clouds.

"Do you remember playing Cloud Castle?" Pym asks.

I open the cloud door and pass through the doorway first. I'm not ready to confess to her how much our little games still mean to me. I want that to be a special moment. Maybe we can play Cloud Castle again, now as adults with a real future together.

We both gasp as we look around at the things piled in the room. I'd half-expected the doors to continue leading to staircases forever, but the cloud door has led us somewhere special. We're in a room stacked wall to wall, floor to ceiling, with magical glittery packages marked FOOD. We will finally eat what people eat. We will finally eat a meal that isn't made of people.

"Do you think it's safe to eat?" Pym asks.

"Of course," I say. "It's food, isn't it?"

She flashes a skeptical smile and kisses me on the cheek before moving toward the nearest wall of packaged foodstuffs. It takes us a few minutes to figure out how to open the packages, then we're tearing them open as fast as we can manage, examining the food before casting it aside. We're too afraid to put any of this stuff in our mouths. The food looks so strange and unfamiliar, but the packages are

NO CHILDREN

so much fun to open.

"Wait," Pym says. "This seems wasteful. For all we know, this is the last food in all of City. We can't burn through our whole supply. Why don't we gather up the food we think looks best and then have a feast? It will be like a wedding feast."

"Our wedding feast?" I ask.

"Our wedding feast," she says.

"You're not mad at me for everything that happened?"

She smiles. "Anything you've done, I've done worse."

We turn back to our separate scavenging, inspecting the foods we've already discarded, opening new packages in hopes of discovering something that looks as familiar as a human heart. After a while, we've stockpiled a heaping mound of foodstuffs on the floor. We're kind of bored of searching too. And hungry.

We sit down cross-legged beside each other and examine the food pyramid. I pick up a round, spongy dark thing that smells like sweat. "Let's both try one at the same time," I say.

Pym nods and picks up a flat, jagged yellow thing speckled on top with tiny crusted teardrops. We raise the human food to our mouths and bite down at the same time.

I chew the spongy dark thing, not enjoying the alien texture at all. The taste is even worse.

We spit out the horrible foodstuffs at the same time, retching and wiping our tongues with our hands.

"This shit is horrible," Pym says.

"I agree. Hold on a moment. I think I'm going to vomit." I stand up and stagger toward a stack of food packages that serves as a wall sectioning off a private little area of the room.

I pull down my pants out of Pym's view. I need to shit real bad.

When I'm done with my business, I pull up my pants and look down at the pile of shit on the floor. There's a piece of paper stuck in the shit. I bend down to see it better.

"What are you doing over there? It smells horrible," Pym calls.

The thing sticking out of my shit is the letter she wrote to me and then chewed up and swallowed right before she was married off to Bill. I pry the letter shard out of my shit and wipe it off on the floor. When it's clean, I read the words, curious to know what fragment of her work chanced survival. I laugh a little to myself. My heart feels good. Alone in this strange room with Pym, with no direction home, life is beautiful.

I return to where she sits beside the pile of inedible crap, wishing we had some hearts or brains to eat.

I hand her this shit-stained scrap of paper that says *I love you*. Rather than a desperate confession or a funny kid thing to say, it feels true this time. It feels like a new beginning.

The Roadkill Quarterback of Heavy Metal High

Chapter One

Danny the werewolf took off his headphones mid-Holy Diver as he walked into first period. The other students were playing the final air guitar notes of Heavy Metal High's Allegiance to Death. He sat at a desk in the back of the classroom beside Barbetta, head cheerleader and girlfriend of Moose Elwood, star quarterback of the football team. The honor roll metalheads sitting near the front of the class started up their usual banter.

"Werewolves suck," said Richie Bratwurst, the fat smartass.

"Watch out, loser," said somebody else, as a spitball zipped past Danny's snout.

Laughter erupted throughout the classroom. Danny pulled his math book from his backpack and opened to a random page. He pretended to study a geometry graph. Ever since Moose Elwood beat him out for the quarterback job during summer training camp three years ago, picking on Danny had become routine. It was the life of a backup, the life of a loser who bore his cross of failure because others enjoyed watching him suffer.

Mr. Ferrell snubbed a cigarette out on his desk and approached the blackboard. "Quiet up, class. Danny's a shame to us all, but your final test is next week and we've still got to cover the mathematics of the hair metal solo."

Danny shivered; his fur reddened. Math was his worst subject. He would be lucky to squeeze by with a D this semester. He couldn't even find the square root of most Black Sabbath songs, something most students had mastered during the first week.

As Mr. Ferrell scribbled musical notes and a stick figure of Satan on the board, Barbetta slipped a note onto Danny's desk.

His heart raced. Barbetta was the most beautiful girl in

school. She had gotten run over by a train on two occasions. Few metalheads mustered the courage to orchestrate one train accident. Surviving two of them made her a school legend. All Danny ever wanted was to be a legend.

Danny unfolded the note and read *You better lose it*.

Lose what, he replied.

Barbetta pressed a tissue to her eyes and passed the note back to him. *Your virginity*.

Everyone in school knew that Danny had never staged a single accident. *Why bother*, he wrote. *I'm waiting for the right time*.

You better do it quick. Moose got in an accident this morning.

Of course he did. He's team captain. It's pre-game ritual.

Moose died this morning.

Danny began to sweat.

Barbetta broke into a crying fit and ran out of the classroom. All of the students faced Danny, glaring at him with their fiercest Danzig grimaces, which they had learned in Facial Education.

Mr. Ferrell broke his chalk and crushed it to dust between the fingers of one of his chain mail gloves. "Danny, this is the third time this week that you've upset a member of the fairer gender. Should I duct tape your mouth again, or can I trust that you'll sit still and fail quietly?"

Danny wiped the sweat from his furry forehead and stared at the note lying on his desk. "Mr. Ferrell, I—"

"Give me that paper," Mr. Ferrell marched down the rows of desks, "there's no note-taking in math class." He swiped the note from the desk and held it up to the fluorescent lights. After he stared at it for over a minute, he crumpled the paper and shoved it in his mouth. He gulped it down and in a low voice said, "A dark day is upon us. Go to the dean's office, Danny. Surely you're responsible for this tragedy."

Chapter Two

The bell rang, announcing the start of second period. Danny fidgeted in the chair across from Dean Hellfrost. The dean clasped her icicle fingers and cracked her knuckles, releasing a cluster of damned souls that floated out of her translucent hands and popped on the stucco ceiling. "I'm sure half the school heard about Moose during passing period, but I still must break the news officially. You realize what this means, don't you?" she said.

Danny scratched at the fur beneath his jersey. He itched all over. His tongue felt like a wad of cotton.

Dean Hellfrost rapped her nails on her desk. "It means you'll have to play in tonight's conference game against Old Time. This has me in a fret, Danny. We've beat the Country Vampires for many consecutive years. Even if Moose Elwood is dead, losing this game would be a huge letdown to him. A real disservice to his memory. So keep him in mind while you're on the field tonight, will you? Which brings me to my next concern. As per league rules, all starters must have engaged in at least one legitimate accident at some point in their high school career prior to taking the field. To the best of my knowledge, you're the only upper classman on the team with zero accidents on your record." She narrowed her cold eyes at Danny. "You're not afraid of getting hurt, are you?"

"N-no mam," Danny said.

"Good," she said. "Life demands pain because pain gives us meaning."

"Y-yes mam."

"You've got until five o'clock to stage a horrific accident, something even Moose wouldn't have dared. Can a werewolf like you accomplish that?"

Danny's head bobbed up and down.

"Then get out of my office. We have a conference to win."

Danny stood and left the dean's office, his shoulders slumped. His eyes welled with tears.

Danny pulled a tissue from the box on the secretary's counter and left the school office.

In the gymnasium, the school band was playing Iron Maiden's Number of the Beast. The noise was quiet in the office, but deathly loud once Danny stepped outside.

The October heat pelted him, but it was nothing compared to last month, when the temperature never fell below 115 degrees. The scorching weather actually relieved Danny now. He could pretend those weren't tears in his eyes. Just sweat.

He saw no sign of the skelecops in the main hallway. They'd probably gone off to smoke pot. Dabbing at his eyes with the tissue, Danny pushed through the door of the men's bathroom. He walked to the far stall and locked himself inside, where he sobbed quietly until a gong sounded. Second period would end in five minutes. He had to collect himself.

His time to stage an accident had pounced upon him like a thunder cat that lashed out more fiercely with every passing minute. He needed to plan something brave and tragic, something splendid and totally metal . . . something greater than the benchwarmer he would always be.

Chapter Three

He made it to history class on time. The other students refrained from their usual taunts. In fact, they completely ignored him as the metalbot, Mr. 666, took attendance and reminisced about the crucifixion of Alice Cooper, which was October's central history lesson.

Ten minutes into third period, feedback reverberated from the intercom. Dean Hellfrost's voice crackled over the wash of static. "Staff and students, I regret to inform you that Moose Elwood, our heroic quarterback, is dead. He passed away this morning after his monster truck collided with two military carriers hauling napalm. This is a sad day for everyone at Heavy Metal High. Benchwarmer Danny has vowed to be ready for tonight's game, so if you see him, give him a swift kick in the ass. Nobody will get in the way of our conference title. The Old Time Country Vampires are going down!"

Mr. 666 unleashed a string of profane beeps and whirrs.

Nerbert Neeb, the team kicker who always sat in the seat closest to the podium because he had an android fetish, slammed his forehead against his desk. "There goes our season," Nerbert groaned.

Hushed banter filled the room until Mr. 666 punched a hole through the dry erase board. "Take this news as a history lesson, class. By the end of the period, I want you to turn in a two page paper on how Alice Cooper would have acted in the face of such adversity." The metalbot kicked the clipboard to a corner of the room and wheeled to its desk.

Danny hung his head. He pinched his furry thigh to distract himself from all his worry. He feared he would start crying again.

He fished a notebook out of his backpack and opened to the first blank page. Pen in hand, he considered all the ways he could approach this paper. He doodled a caricature of himself in the margin and then scribbled a pack of redneck vampires preparing to suck his blood.

A spitball pelted Danny in the face. The class sniggered as he wiped it off. He lowered his head, choosing to put all his energy into writing so that he could ignore the teasing. He wrote:

The accident comes in many forms. I have never been crucified, but that doesn't mean I haven't experienced my share of mishaps. What Alice Cooper never told us is that some of us who are considered lazy or dumb or cowardly for abstaining from real accidents are actually none of those things. For the ones like us, life is just one big accident. Anyway, Alice Cooper's real name was Vincent Damon Fournier. Fuck him, and fuck his crucifixion. Ronnie James Dio never died, so why did Alice? His real name was Ronnie James Padavona, but that is such a better name that Vincent Damon Fournier. Ronnie James is immortal. He knows what it means to be the underdog. In the music video for Holy Diver, he teaches us more about life than Alice Cooper's crappy crucifixion ever will. In Ronnie, I find strength. I know that someday I will also ride the tiger.

Overexcited and absorbed in his work, Danny raised both hands in classic devil horns and shouted, "Dio, motherfuckers!"

For this, he was promptly dismissed from the classroom. In the small-minded world of Heavy Metal High, everybody hated Dio. The history books brainwashed students. They claimed Dio's entire career was a scourge to metal history, especially his time as Black Sabbath front man. Danny knew better. Heaven and Hell, Mob Rules, and Dehumanizer were all classic albums. In fact, he hated most non-Dio Sabbath material. He thought Ozzy Osbourne was an ass goblin.

He stood outside the classroom, counting cigarette burns on the black door. Somebody had graffitied a poor rendition of Skeletor. After USA Network stopped airing He-Man and the Masters of the Universe in 1990, Skeletor took a demotion from Evil Lord of Destruction to head honcho of Heavy Metal High's security staff. He was a wrathful tactician, often tempting students to commit crimes that would have otherwise gone uncommitted. Dean Hellfrost had already threatened to fire him three times this year for the brutal punishments he frequently dealt to innocent students. Rape and pillage may have been effective in his quest to conquer Eternia, but they provided a less than ideal backdrop for the academic environment.

Danny sniggered at the image on the door. The graffiti artist had stenciled two gargoyles jabbing their penises into Skeletor's eye sockets. At the bottom, in crimson scrawl, one word: SKELEFUCKED.

Fortunately, Danny always managed to avoid encounters with Skeletor. He'd heard rumors about what the head security guard did to werewolves, and being turned into lycanthropic meatloaf by a megalomaniacal skeleton ranked very low on his list of things to do before he died.

The bell rang, startling Danny, forcing a hairball of worry out of his mouth. He scampered away, hiccupping and coughing up hairballs all the way to his next class.

Chapter Four

Fourth period meant English, Danny's favorite subject. Seniors spent their final year of English studying the complete works of Marquis de Sade, but Danny's teacher had fallen sick the week before and they'd had the same substitute since Monday. The substitute was a G.G. Allin impersonator. Whenever a student asked a question about their readings, the substitute pulled at his reverse Hitler mustache and said, "The Marquis can bite it."

Today, Danny arrived before any of his peers. The Allin impersonator was naked and slumped over the teacher's desk, a syringe in his arm, a dead roman candle dangling from his asshole.

Danny sat as far from the substitute as possible and read the words on the blackboard. *Write a ballad to honor the memory of Moose Elwood. Don't turn it in. Nobody wants to read your crap.*

Considering the substitute probably couldn't spell his own name, Danny figured another teacher must have slipped in and written this on the board.

Most of the kids showed up a few minutes after the late bell. Being on time hardly mattered when the only authority figure was a junky.

Barbetta took the seat beside Danny. He glanced over. Streaks of mascara ran down to her chin. His heart thudded. A girl as beautiful as Barbetta would never fall for a werewolf like Danny. The only other werewolves at Heavy Metal High took up space in the special education program, and although he only resembled them in physical appearance, everyone made the same cruel jokes about him. No, they made crueler jokes about Danny.

As she did in first period, Barbetta passed a note to

Danny. He undid the pentagram-folded paper and flattened it against his desk. *Need help with your accident?*

Danny gulped. He looked over at Barbetta. She winked at him. He took out his pen. He didn't know what to say. She hardly acknowledged that he existed. Why suddenly offer to help him now? *It's all planned out. Nobody will believe what I'm gonna do*, he lied.

When Barbetta returned the note, he looked around the room. Most of the students appeared to be absorbed in completing the assignment. Apparently, Moose's death shook them so badly that they would do anything, even schoolwork, to honor the fallen hero.

Sexy!

Danny rubbed his eyes to ensure that he wasn't seeing wrong, that Barbetta had really written *s-e-x-y* in her girly scrawl. He slipped on his headphones. Rainbow's Run with the Wolf, from the '76 album Rising, filled his fuzzy ears. He stared at the note until the lunch gong sounded.

Sexy!

Chapter Five

Danny was zipping up his backpack in the crowded hall, his brown lunch sack clenched between his teeth, when Barbetta approached.

He flung his backpack over his shoulders and squeezed the paper bag in his hands to prevent the nervous tremors running through him. He worried that his fur might look uncombed, but wasn't it always uncombed? No one ever approached Danny with anything nice to say. He figured Barbetta wanted to tell him not to ruin the football season, at least for the sake of her dead boyfriend.

"Hi," she said, flipping hair out of her face.

"How are you?" Danny said. "I mean, after Moose's accident."

Barbetta shrugged. "We all have to die sometime."

"You seemed pretty upset earlier."

"I never pass up an opportunity for a good cry. I like drama."

"You mean you like acting?"

"You're not very bright, are you?"

"I guess that's what you wanted to tell me."

"Not at all! I want to show you something. I'm sure the accident you're planning is great, but I think this will help."

Danny blushed. He wanted to confess that he had nothing planned, that he desperately needed Barbetta's assistance. Alone, he was a hopeless cause. "Everything will work out fine without you. I have everything I need. It's going to be awesome, thanks."

He started to turn away, his stomach growling at the thought of the pork fries and sausage sandwich in his lunch sack.

"Don't bullshit me," Barbetta said. "If you fuck up tonight, the other kids will crucify you, and Skeletor will do something even worse. You need me."

"Won't the rest of the cheer squad miss you?"

Barbetta sighed and took him by the mane. She pulled him further from the yard where students ate lunch, away from the drone of a shitty black metal band.

She led him into an open classroom and locked the door behind them.

She pressed against Danny and puckered her lips for a kiss. Unfortunately for Danny, he reacted in the way all werewolves do when confronted with unexpected closeness: he bit.

He pulled away from her.

He spit Barbetta's face onto the floor. She raised her hands to her bloody skull and moaned. Danny picked chunks of flesh and hair from between his fangs. He had never felt so humiliated in his life.

Something was lodged in the back of his throat. He coughed. Barbetta's nose plopped to the ground. "I'm so sorry." He reached for her but then withdrew, tucking his hands in his pockets, afraid to touch her. "Let me take you to the health center."

"My face!"

Danny backed against the door. Surely the school would sentence him to death for mangling the lead cheerleader. "I'm sure they can put it back on."

"I've always wanted to see my skull," Barbetta said, still hiding her new face from Danny. "Reach into my purse and fetch my mirror. I want to know how I look."

No girl had ever asked Danny to get something out of her purse. It seemed an intimate thing to do. Her purse lay beside her face flesh. He picked up the purse and pulled out a mirror studded with pink and black jewels. "Here you go," he said.

Barbetta took the mirror. Danny grimaced as she removed her hands from her face to inspect herself. "I am finally beautiful," she said.

"I always thought you were beautiful," Danny said, although he liked her much better when flesh covered her skull. "What was it you wanted to show me?"

"Oh, that doesn't matter anymore," she tilted her head to inspect herself from a different angle, "I'm sure your accident will be wonderful. I never dreamed a man, er—werewolf, would bite my face off. It's so fucking sexy."

Danny swallowed back vomit. Whatever ointments or makeup had covered Barbetta's face were making him sick. He wanted to run out of the classroom but realized what a lifetime opportunity he'd been thrown.

Barbetta took her purse from Danny and scooped her face off the floor. She stuck her face and mirror in the purse and grinned fiendishly. "I'll make you a deal."

"W-what kind of deal?"

She ran a finger down the center of his jersey. "If you beat Old Time tonight, I'll give you the time of your life after the game."

"T-that's very kind of you—" but Barbetta pushed around him and left him alone in the classroom, where he stayed for the remainder of lunch, eating his sausage sandwich and pork fries, contemplating the terrible fortune life had suddenly thrown his way.

Chapter Six

Biology and Facial Education passed without any notable disasters, except that he definitively failed a pop quiz on the tongue of Gene Simmons. Nobody spoke to Danny and he didn't spot Barbetta in the hall between classes. He felt everyone watching him and whispering behind his back. Of course, they anticipated his accident. He considered visiting Doom McCray, his head coach, or an academic counselor for advice, but he knew they would tell him the same old thing . . . how conceiving a wreck is a personal matter and any advice from staff members made the school liable in the event of death. He needed to pull himself up by the bootstraps. He didn't want to conjure any doubt about his ability to lead Heavy Metal High to victory.

After seventh period, Danny walked out to the bus lot and got on bus #34. He plopped down in an empty seat near the front. The faux leather scorched his back and thighs. Although the school bus had no air conditioning, Danny preferred the heat to the company of his peers and the brooding ferocity of his father. Along the ride, he listened to Elf, the gods of blues rock and Ronnie James' first band.

Dan Sr. was a sullen man and a drunk. He wrote for the sports page of the local paper and occasionally picked up freelance work. When Danny's mother died of breast cancer during his freshman year, Dan Sr. lost all interest in his son. He made arrangements with the paper to write his articles from home, which he did during the four or five hours he managed to stay sober each day. Since Danny typically arrived home around four, he had not seen his father sober on a school day in three years.

But when he walked through the door on this unusual Friday, his father greeted him with a big lycanthropic hug.

Danny detected no alcohol on his father's clothes or breath.

"Dean Hellfrost called me this morning. Congratulations, son. I always knew you'd be a champ." His fur smelled sour, his liver was probably too damaged to ever be repaired, but at least he was alive for this moment.

"But dad, I—"

"Take it to state," the sallow, yellow-haired werewolf marched around the living room, "take it to state, my boy!"

Danny tried to recall the last time he saw his father so animated. It saddened him to think that he would shrink back into alcoholic despair if Heavy Metal lost the game.

"I need to come up with an accident," he said.

Dan Sr. paused in mid-celebration. "An accident? You're seventeen years old and you haven't staged an accident? Where have you wasted your time? This is the most important day of your life! If Violet saw what a dumbass I'd raised our son to be."

Danny's father started to shake all over. He ran out of the room. How the potbellied werewolf lost faith so fast totally crushed Danny. He took off his backpack and left the house as the cry of breaking glass yielded to the howls of his father.

Out on the sidewalk, he watched car after car pass him by. He could jump in front of an SUV, but half the players on his team had already done that. The role of quarterback demanded more flair.

He was so stupid. He'd been so close to regaining his father's love, but within minutes of standing in the same room together, everything returned to disrepair. "I guess that's the natural way of things," Danny said.

The absurdity of hearing himself say such a pitiful thing struck a chord in his mind. If he was too much of a loser to perform an epic accident, then fuck football and Heavy Metal, fuck accidents and all other forms of life. Wasn't it the great fortune of every creature on the planet to be born inherently worthless? He resolved to give the metalheads a suicide nobody would ever forget.

Chapter Seven

He went inside the house again, heading straight for the garage. He thought about Barbetta. He doubted that snuffing himself out would make her give a rat's ass, but he no longer cared.

He switched on the garage light and found a chainsaw and some rope. He climbed inside his father's truck.

He slipped his walkman from the pocket of his cutoff jeans and plugged it into the stereo. He took the spare key from a plastic clip on the sun visor.

He chose Sunset Superman from Dio's Dream Evil to kick off his farewell soundtrack. The rest of the mix consisted of songs from Rainbow's Rising, Black Sabbath's Heaven and Hell, and the entirety of Holy Diver, the greatest album of all time.

He fashioned a noose and turned on the truck before slipping the rope over his head. To die by the dual means of choking and decapitation would require expert timing.

The chainsaw sat beside him on the bench-style seat. He ran his fingers over the blade, fearless and without any regrets. He laughed a bit, thinking how everything in life worked out so strangely. He never viewed himself as the suicidal type, although maybe that was how others saw him. Danny never felt safe in his judgments of himself.

Petting the chainsaw, he lost himself in the scripture of Sunset Superman. "*A shadow without a name, but when he wakes up in the morning, he just won't know he was a hero . . . trying to hide his burning heart before somebody cuts it all away.*"

Tightening the noose, he lost himself in the crunchy sweet guitar of Craig Goldy.

It felt like the truck was rising, levitating beyond the

roof of the garage to meet the black pixels of space.

The noose constricted his breathing.

He rasped for air. He struggled to lift the chainsaw. *So heavy, oh so heavy.* The blade spun round and round.

Sunset Superman!

The door leading to the garage opened. Danny's father stood in the doorway. He shouted, but Danny heard nothing, for the music and the chainsaw were so loud. He knew he must prevent his father from foiling his suicide.

His father staggered toward the truck and pried at the driver's side door. The drunken man balled his hands into fists and punched the window, first with a left and quickly following with a right, but the glass held strong under the drunk man's blows. Danny balanced the whining chainsaw between his legs and shifted the truck into reverse.

He slammed on the gas pedal. The truck pummeled through the garage door. Danny loosened the rope around his neck. He breathed deeply, relief filling his lungs. He killed the chainsaw's motor and sped out of the neighborhood to the cue of Sabbath's Die Young, heading toward the highway. The bustle of rush hour could ensure him a glorious death.

Chapter Eight

He hit the highway going ninety and only pushed it harder from there. The tape player did a weird thing. It stopped playing Die Young and switched to Dio's Holy Diver. Some sort of ghostly transference. Real metal shit.

Danny couldn't fuss with the tape right then. He only learned to drive recently and he had a chainsaw between his legs.

He merged into the middle lane and honked at a puttering Chevy. He sped up to within a foot of the truck's bumper and swerved into the left lane, too late to avoid forcing a black VW bug into oncoming traffic. Danny overcorrected, briefly returning to the center lane before losing control and following the bug through a web of southbound vehicles.

Out of fear, he let the chainsaw slip from between his legs. Falling to the floorboard, it quickly spun out of control and severed his legs at the ankles.

Danny screamed. He realized he would have his accident now, but it was no longer a prize he wanted. Did he ever want it in the first place? He no longer knew.

He followed the bug as it bee-lined against traffic at nearly one-hundred miles per hour. Danny didn't realize those little piece of shit cars got up so fast.

He was losing blood. He felt the blood puddle reach the bottoms of his pants. It soaked his shins and low-hanging knees. All to the nightmare hymn of Holy Diver.

When the blood filled the cab up to his neck, Danny undid his seatbelt. With his left hand, he fumbled around for the window knob-a-majig, then remembered it was broken. He returned his left hand to the wheel and racked his brain for ways to avoid drowning in his own blood.

The blood rose to his chin, his mouth, his eyes. He squinted through red now. The black VW looked like a real insect.

All Danny could think was, *I must squash it. Squash that bug.*

He slumped down in his chair until his right stump pressed against the gas pedal, accelerating his father's truck above one-hundred miles per hour. He crept up on the bug and soon flattened the car into a dark pancake.

He let out a scream and lost the last of his breath. In a final desperate attempt to get free of the truck, Danny flailed his arms at the chainsaw on the floorboard. The chainsaw buzzed his arms from his torso and propelled his hands out the side windows in opposite directions. They stuck there, like the truck had arms.

Danny no longer had control of the truck and couldn't reach the brake pedal. He glanced in the rearview mirror.

Holy diver!

The flattened Beetle had ballooned into a real six-legged insect and it followed him.

The chainsaw floated through the truck's blood-filled cab. It sat in the passenger seat. The chainsaw leaned over and turned up the volume on the stereo. Holy Diver blared through the crimson flood. *You've been down so long in the midnight sea. . . .*

The glass-and-tin insect scuttled down the highway on rubber legs. They were still heading into oncoming traffic and cars in the carpool lane had to swerve to avoid them. Unable to steer, Danny stared at the chainsaw and said, in muffled underwater screams, "What do we do?"

A steel grin split open on the blade. The chainsaw stuck out a tongue that resembled a squid tentacle. "We crash," the chainsaw said. The smile disappeared as the chainsaw leapt across the seat.

Danny ducked. The chainsaw narrowly missed giving him a fast lane lobotomy and sheared off his left ear. For a few photo-still seconds, the ear floated in front of Danny's face like a hairy seahorse.

The chainsaw broke into a smile again. It flapped that awful tongue and laughed and foamed yellow bubbles from the steely mouth. The truck rolled end over end.

As the insect-car scuttled by, its driver—a private detective type in a tweed suit, true Eurotrash—flipped Danny off and yelled, "Volkswagens for life, motherfucker!"

Danny choked down gallons of his own blood, but the blood rushed out at an incredible rate, and soon he died.

Chapter Nine

"Wake up, kid."

The chainsaw prodded Danny's side as they pulled into Heavy Metal High's parking lot.

The dead werewolf opened his eyes. Somehow he'd ended up in the passenger seat. The chainsaw must have driven from the scene of the accident all the way to the school.

Danny's eyelids felt heavy. He wanted to sleep but knew it was a bad idea. Without arms, he couldn't feel for a heartbeat or a pulse. How the hell did he survive his own death?

"What's going on?" he asked the chainsaw.

The chainsaw killed the engine. It slammed its blade against the steering wheel again and again, setting off the horn. Danny leaned back and stared out the window at his severed right arm.

"What's going on?"

"You're dead, kid," the chainsaw said.

"Can we turn the radio on?" Danny said, missing Ronnie Dio's voice. He kept gazing out the window at his severed arm.

"You've got a game to play."

"How can I open the door without my arms?"

"You'll die if you open these doors."

"I'm already dead." Danny sulked in his seat. "How can I play in tonight's game?"

The chainsaw sighed. "This is your new body, kid. Get used to it."

"But there's no way I can throw a football without any arms!"

"This is your body. You're in control."

"How do you know? Who are you?" Danny wasn't sure if he should trust this chainsaw. After all, it had cut off all his limbs and caused him to wreck his dad's truck. But isn't that what he wanted?

"That's not important now," the chainsaw said, gesturing toward the cars parked around them. "Check it out."

Barbetta and the rest of the cheer squad had approached the truck. They stood in a semicircle, clapping their hands and screaming while jumping up and down.

"Awesome accident, Danny!"

Danny gasped. It didn't make any sense at all. Just this morning, Moose had died in an accident. How could a loser lycanthrope like himself possibly survive death? The last metalhead to pull off that stunt was Goyle Flex back in '68, after he threw the most legendary touchdown pass in Heavy Metal High's history, the Batball, in which the football transformed into a bat and bit the heads off of five Old Time Country Vampires. It was still the greatest massacre in school history.

Since that game, Heavy Metal and Old Time competed in every league championship, but mass slaughters were now strictly forbidden before the fourth quarter.

Danny gulped. He might have died, but that didn't mean the Country Vampires couldn't massacre his ass with their bloodsucking hillbilly powers. At seventeen, sitting in his father's wrecked truck, which was filled like a fish tank with his own blood, he wondered how his life could possibly get any worse. Then he saw the beautiful, skeleton-faced Barbetta. She made him feel even more like a furry slab of wasted meat.

"Let's hit the locker room, kid," the chainsaw said, turning on the truck and returning Ronnie James Dio's archangelic yowls to the cab. "Game time's in one hour and you're still learning to control this new body. Now raise some horns for the girlies."

Danny shrugged. "But I don't know how," he said, then watched, mystified, as his arms, attached to the sides of the car like extended, flesh-covered rearview mirrors, raised their hands into fists that balled up to form the classic devil horns. The cheerleaders returned the gesture.

Chapter Ten

Coach Doom McCray slapped Danny's tailgate as the dead werewolf stalled outside the hall to the locker room, trying to figure out some way that he could fit his new truck body inside. "Looks like you had yourself a fine accident, Danny," Doom McCray said. "You might never blossom into a Moose, but I'm glad to see it's not all hopeless for a late-blooming fuckup like yourself. C'mon, go get suited up."

Upon entering the stadium grounds, the chainsaw had gone silent, leaving Danny to maneuver his auto body without assistance. Now he didn't know what to do. He peered out the back window and grinned sheepishly at the head coach. "Coach Doom, I don't know if I can fit through this hallway."

Doom pulled at the corners of his handlebar mustache. "It does appear that you've beefed up, put on some serious muscle. Not juicing, are you?"

"No, sir. My accident did this to me."

"Good to hear. I always believed quarterbacks bred purely on accidents were the best leaders."

"I-I hope I don't let the team down, sir," Danny stammered.

For a second time, Coach Doom slapped Danny's tailgate. "Remember, if we lose, there's no one to blame but you."

The coach walked around Danny and vanished down the concrete hall, whistling the Heavy Metal Anthem as he entered the locker room.

Unable to conceive a better way to get inside, Danny clenched his hands into fists and swung with all his force, pummeling the concrete into dust. He threw punches all down the hallway until finally he squeezed into the locker room. About half the team was suiting up, including the all-state Siamese twin linebackers, Bert and Bartholomew Spielman. Everyone went silent as Danny drove to the last row of lockers and began turning his lock to the four digits of the combination.

He reached an arm into the locker and pulled out his helmet, jersey, and the rest of his uniform.

That he could no longer wear any of this gear quickly dawned on him. The helmet seemed unimportant. His limbless body was now protected by one ton of manly truck power. Nor did the pants or cleats matter, for he walked on wheels. However, he wanted—nay, needed—his jersey to play. The rules required it, for one. Also, he loved that number thirteen.

Danny went into reverse and headed for Coach Doom's office. He kicked into four-wheel drive, wheeled up the steps, and knocked on the door.

"Come in," Coach Doom yelled.

Danny opened the door. It was impossible for him to actually fit inside the office, so he stood in the doorway, shifting his weight from wheel to wheel.

Doom glanced up from the playbook that sat on the table between the other coaches, the waterboy, and himself. "What is it, Danny?" he said.

"Sir, I can't fit into my uniform."

"Is that so?" The coach spat tobacco onto the floor. "I suppose Dodge makes a sturdy frame. It'd tear a jersey to shreds. What do you think, fellas? I think it's only the number that matters. What number do you wear, Danny? Thirteen?"

"Yes, thirteen," Danny said.

"That's right, all in the number," said Krallick, the assistant coach.

Coach Doom turned back to the playbook. "Waterboy, fish up some of that crimson spray paint and slather a real menacing thirteen on Danny's hood."

The waterboy bowed his head, got up from his chair, and rummaged through the cabinets beneath the rows of coffee pots that gargled on the counter, fixing their single red eyes on Danny.

The waterboy pulled out the spray paint can and shut the cabinet. He approached Danny, shaking the can and keeping his face hidden beneath a cobwebbed tangle of greasy dreadlocks.

Danny closed his eyes when the first layer of paint hit him. It felt cold and slick on his hood, but he realized this meant that not only could he control his body, he was also gaining a sense of feeling. The paint job ended soon enough. Danny inched down the staircase backwards. "Lookin' good, wolf boy," Krallick called from the office. "Nice accident."

Since he had no other preparations to make, Danny saw no reason to return to his locker. Instead, he revved his engine and started for the pig pit, where the team gathered before each game to ask the metal gods for a brutal victory. A few of his teammates already knelt in the pit. They suckled on the pig's feet protruding from the walls. Above them, Goyle Flex's skeleton hung upside-down on a cross made of Country Vampire tongues. Danny suddenly felt giddy. Tonight, he realized, he had a chance to fulfill his childhood dream of being a star player. If he somehow found a way to honor the legend of Goyle Flex in tonight's game, his own reputation might be set for life.

Danny's hood opened up and a huge furry tongue unraveled from the engine. It licked at the pig's feet and they tasted good to Danny.

Chapter Eleven

The Old Time Country Vampires won the coin toss and chose to receive the ball first. The special teams units took the field as Back in Black blared from the massive speakers lining the home side of the stadium. Cheerleaders on each side kicked up their legs and flashed the crowd, all part of their usual kickoff routines.

Despite the cheers he received from the girls out in the parking lot, none of Danny's teammates had spoken to him. He figured they must be suspicious of his accident, maybe even jealous. Whatever the case, he hoped to prove them wrong soon enough.

Danny drowned out all the surrounding noise by adjusting the volume knob on his radio. He listened to Holy Diver on repeat. It soothed the machine heart that beat nervously beneath his hood.

Kickoff!

The ball sailed across the field. The kick returner waved for a fair catch and caught the ball just shy of the twenty yard line. A referee blew a whistle, beckoning Old Time's offense and Heavy Metal's defense onto the field as the special teams units rushed off.

Both teams huddled about ten yards away on opposite sides from where the referee placed the football. Danny stood on the sideline, trying to forget how much the next few hours would change his life.

Chapter Twelve

In the commentary booth:

Biff Bifferson: Here we are at Goyle Stadium for the thirty-first consecutive conference championship between the Heavy Metal High Death Crusaders and the Old Time Country Vampires. It's been a tragic day for the Death Crusaders. Just this morning, they lost star quarterback Moose Elwood in a fatal accident. Moose's legend will live on, but all of us will miss him. Replacing Moose at quarterback is Danny the werewolf. Although Danny has only played in scrimmage games, it appears that he showed up prepared to throw down the horns tonight, fresh from a mighty fine accident. And speaking of tragic days, my wife of five years walked out on me this morning. She insists that I drink too much. I say what does she know. I'm a sportswriter with a bad back. My wife, she—

Beelzebub: Biff Bifferson, can we focus on the game?

Biff Bifferson: Oh, right. It's just my wife. I can't stop thinking about her, so of course I slipped a few nips of the grain before coming in, if you know what I mean. You know what I mean, don't you?

Beelzebub: Old Time won the coin toss and called for a fair catch at their own eighteen yard line. The Country Vampires' offense and Death Crusaders' defense have taken to the field.

Biff Bifferson: By the way, did you catch Maiden's tour dates? I swear, Bruce puts the DICK in Dickinson.

Beelzebub: The Vampires are set at the line of scrimmage. It's a quick snap. The handoff goes to running back Turbo Ginn. Ginn takes it for a short gain.

Biff Bifferson: Like that pro-STD metal band, Hell's Crabs. Somebody should tell those cocksuckers that syphilis is never metal.

Beelzebub: Shutup, Biff Bifferson. Starting quarterback for Old Time is Whiskey Nash, who broke Goyle Flex's state record for passing touchdowns this season. I'll tell you, I've been watching Nash all season and this kid is the real deal. Other starters for the Vampires include running back Turbo, the twelve foot tall bruiser, and wide receiver Marcus Aurelius. Nobody else on the offense scores enough on or off the field for anyone listening in Radioland to care.

Biff Bifferson: What about that Heavy Metal defense, Bub? Tell 'em about those whippersnappers.

Beelzebub: Leading the defense are the Siamese twin linebackers, Bert and Bartholomew Spielman. Let's get back to the action on the field.

Biff Bifferson: If I hadn't been wrong about these things before, I'd swear that duo's going pro.

Beelzebub: What a pass! Whiskey Nash connects with Marcus Aurelius for a twenty yard gain.

Biff Bifferson: Fuck professionalism.

Beelzebub: Biff Bifferson, you can't say that on the air. First and ten on the thirty-eight yard line.

THE ROADKILL QUARTERBACK OF HEAVY METAL HIGH

Biff Bifferson: There goes Turbo Ginn! Fuck some chickens, boy!

Beelzebub: The Spielman twins make the tackle. Old Time has first and ten on the fifty yard line.

Biff Bifferson: I swear, this year's Country Vampires are going to give the Death Crusaders a serious run for their drug money.

Beelzebub: We can't talk about drugs on the air either.

Biff Bifferson: Beer money, then.

Beelzebub: They're minors. They can't drink beer.

Biff Bifferson: Go fuck yourself, you old fly.

Beelzebub: The game, Biff Bifferson. Focus on the game.

Biff Bifferson: This one is bound to be a classic. Classically bad, maybe. We've yet to see what kind of chops this Danny Werewolf character is packing. Except on his face!

Beelzebub: Please, Biff Bifferson. Refrain from making fun of the werewolf's sideburns.

Chapter Thirteen

Danny watched from the sideline as Turbo Ginn concluded the Country Vampires' first drive with a long breakaway touchdown run.

An orange number six lit up on the scoreboard for the visiting team. After they kicked the extra point, it changed to a seven.

The Death Crusaders didn't gain much on the kickoff return, giving the offense a start around their own fifteen yard line.

The crowd went wild as Danny took the field for the first time in his high school career. He wondered what they thought of him. Most had probably placed bets that he'd fuck everything up. At the same time, he looked badass in the blood-filled truck.

He huddled with his teammates and called for a handoff up the middle to Byronius "Speed Goblin" Alexander. Along with Moose Elwood, Byronius had been a major factor in Heavy Metal's current undefeated season. He'd rushed for more yards and touchdowns than anyone in a decade.

Danny lined up behind the center, Biggy Pie, and prepared to take the snap. "Hut, hut, hike!"

The ball slapped against his hands, which had to stretch all the way around to the front grill. He pivoted and made the handoff to Byronius, who got stuffed at the line of scrimmage.

The next play was an outside pitch to Byronius. Again, the running back went nowhere.

On third down with ten yards to go, Coach Doom signaled in a curl pass. Danny gulped. This would be his first passing attempt ever.

Although Danny had several players he could throw to on this play, he already anticipated getting the ball to wide receiver Mickey Styx. Nobody could pull in a pass, no matter how wild or sloppy, like Styx.

Biggy Pie tapped Danny's side mirror as they went up to the ball. "Don't fuck this up," Biggy said.

Danny sank down in his driver's seat and took a deep breath. *Don't fuck this up. Don't fuck this up.*

Suddenly, he felt nauseated. "Hut," he said, followed by rapid-fire hiccups. He belched and had to swallow down some vomit. "Hike!"

He dropped back to pass. He knew he was telegraphing to the defense that he intended throwing the ball to Mickey Styx, but they would've expected as much anyway. Danny waited for Styx to break away from the cornerback covering him. He squealed on his tires as two Vampires broke through the offensive line.

Clueless as to what he should do, Danny flung a high and wild pass far down the field. He held his breath as the ball soared toward the end zone. Just as he thought he'd overthrown it, Mickey Styx leaped into the air and made a miraculous one-handed catch, tagging down the toes of both feet before crashing into the goalpost.

The Heavy Metal fans roared.

Danny had thrown his first touchdown! He was going to be a hero!

But first he needed to vomit.

Chapter Fourteen

As the kicker nailed the extra point, Danny's teammates congratulated him on the sideline. They patted his hood and tailgate and said things like "Awesome job!" and "Fuck yeah, were-bro!"

The cheerleaders turned his name into a chant and the crowd joined in. They loved him.

Everybody loved him!

The game had just begun; they were tied at seven, but Danny was already a hero. Even Coach Doom came over to personally congratulate him.

Within the blood-filled cab, Danny nodded his head and smiled as Coach Doom pumped his fists in the air and returned his attention to the game.

He hardly got a moment to recover from all the positive attention because on the very first play, the Country Vampires' star quarterback, Whiskey Nash, fumbled the ball when the Siamese linebackers sacked him. The twins recovered the fumble.

"Offense, on the field!" Coach Doom shouted. "Fuckin' kick their little bitch asses!"

Danny and the rest of the offense stormed the field.

In the huddle, all eyes fixed on Danny. It was up to him to call the play this time. "Alright, I want an end-around to Styx on three." He clapped his hands to break the huddle, but everyone stared blank-eyed at him.

"Bullshit," said Biggie Pie.

"Yeah man, their defense is too quick. Trick plays won't work on them. They'll see that shit from a mile away," said Mickey Styx.

"Fine." Danny cleared his throat. "Let Byronius smash it up the hole."

"Send 'er deep!" Coach Doom yelled from the sideline.

Byronius shook his head. "Coach called for us to go deep. It worked the first time. You better listen to what he says."

Danny opened his mouth to call for a deep pass, but the referee blew a whistle and threw a yellow flag.

The referee ran to the center of the field and announced, "Delay of game on the offense."

Another ref picked up the ball and moved it back five yards.

"Nice going, dipshit," Biggie Pie told Danny as the team re-huddled.

Danny ignored him, intent on getting the ball snapped in time. "Alright, I want Styx lined up wide right. On set, you, Byronius, motion left. Both of you run five yard curls."

Mickey Styx and Byronius looked at him doubtfully.

"They'll be blitzing heavy because they know I'm inexperienced, and with you two lined up out in the flats, the secondary will fall back, playing it safe to prevent a big play."

Mickey's eyes flashed and he nodded. "Leaving the middle wide open."

"Exactly," Danny said. "Ready, break!"

The Death Crusaders broke their huddle and jogged to the line of scrimmage.

"Down," Danny snarled. "Set."

He revved his engine as Byronius motioned left. The defense adjusted accordingly.

Seconds before Byronius hit the line of scrimmage, Danny shouted, "Hike!"

Danny dropped back deeper in the pocket than he needed to, giving the defense the impression that he was looking long.

The offensive line was losing ground to the blitzing

front seven, but Styx and Byronius had cut in harmoniously. They were wide open. Coverage had dropped back exactly how Danny expected.

He drilled Styx in the chest with the ball. Styx could have run for an easy additional ten yards, if the impact of the ball hadn't knocked him off his feet. Regardless, the pass picked up ten yards.

Back in the huddle, Styx rubbed his chest. "Damn, Danny. You throw short passes harder than Moose."

Danny flashed a toothsome grin before calling the same route again. "Only this time, it's a fullback smash up the hole."

The fullback, Steamboat Larry, was a rock-hard two-hundred-and-fifty pound Irish boy compacted into a five-seven frame. He lived in Old Time's district, but Heavy Metal had recruited him for his brawn and his brains. Steamboat Larry could recite the lyrics to every metal song ever written, even the unrecorded ones. The dude was a telepathic genius in the body of a ripped bulldog.

They lined up at the ball. On cue, Byronius went through his motions. The secondary crept up and the linebackers stepped back, anticipating a repeat of the previous play. Beating a defense was as easy as outsmarting them. Even without his truck body, Danny could have done this all day long.

Steamboat Larry pounded the ball for a six yard gain, earning Heavy Metal a first down.

On the next play, Danny threw a shovel pass to Byronius, who juked and spun for a twelve yard gain. The crowd started up a chant of "Speed . . . Goblin! Speed . . . Goblin!" They pounded their feet on the bleachers, sending up a cacophonous roar of thunder.

Heavy Metal had crossed the fifty yard line.

With another first and ten, Danny hit the tight end on a quick slant. Then they did it again, picking up four to five yards each pass.

On third down with a short yard to go, Coach Doom called in a Hail Mary. He wanted Byronius, Steamboat Larry, the tight end, and both wide receivers all running deep, which would leave only the front five to protect Danny from the defense. He took this as a sign that Coach Doom trusted him now.

The ball was snapped and Danny dropped back. They had double coverage on Mickey Styx and a lone corner on the second receiver. A linebacker picked up the tight end, leaving only one safety to cover Byronius and Steamboat Larry.

Byronius flew down the left side of the field while Steamboat Larry tromped down the right like a stampeding rhinoceros. The safety fell off Styx to cover Byronius with little success. Byronius blew by the safety.

Danny scanned the field. Steamboat Larry was open, but he didn't have the best hands. He'd have to throw between coverage to hit Styx and the second receiver was more of a decoy than an actual target. But did he have the accuracy to hit Byronius from nearly half a field away? The offensive line crumbled and the defense barreled through. Spinning on his wheels, Danny launched an off-kilter bullet toward the Speed Goblin's anticipated trajectory. The pass hit him in perfect stride.

Touchdown!

The gong sounded, signifying the end of the first quarter. Heavy Metal was leading 14-7 and Danny had thrown two touchdown passes. He felt greatness in his blood.

For the first time since the game began, Danny paused and listened to the music that was playing. He couldn't believe his ears. Holy Diver blared from the loudspeakers.

Chapter Fifteen

The Old Time Country Vampires scored a field goal on their first drive of the second quarter, and then surprised the Heavy Metal Death Crusaders with an onside kick. The Vampires recovered the ball and ran it back for a touchdown, taking the lead and bringing the score to 14-17 before Heavy Metal's offense took to the field.

Under Danny's command, Heavy Metal controlled the ball and the clock on three long, pass-heavy drives that each led to scores. In addition to his three passing touchdowns in the second, the defense ran back an interception. With a halftime score of 42-17, the game was looking like a blowout. Even in the heydays of Goyle Flex, games against Old Time were always neck and neck, but today, Heavy Metal was untouchable.

While his teammates jogged to the locker room for halftime, Danny drove over to the bleachers to look for his father, but the old werewolf was nowhere to be seen.

Barbetta waved and blew him a kiss. He smiled and waved back, but returned his searching gaze to the bleachers. He couldn't think about her until the game was over. Maybe his father was getting a hotdog at the concession stand, or using the bathroom. There were a lot of reasons why he would not be in the bleachers during halftime. *Forget about him,* he thought. *He's just a deadbeat anyway.*

When his teammates emerged from the locker room, Danny sped over to meet them in the pig pit, trying to forget about his father and Barbetta. Heavy Metal had been untouchable in the first half, but the game was not over yet. There remained two full quarters of play. Danny had to stay focused. He could still fuck everything up. Licking salty pig's feet was just the thing he needed to get back into game mode.

The third quarter dragged on longer than the first two. Heavy Metal played conservatively on offense, scoring only once. The defense continued shutting down Old Time. The Vampires went three and out most possessions. They racked up four turnovers in the third quarter alone.

Danny felt good to be on the winning side of a beatdown for once in his life.

Chapter Sixteen

In the commentary booth:

Beelzebub: Heading into the fourth quarter, the score is 49-17, Heavy Metal in the lead. The last thing anyone expected was for this championship to be a blowout in Heavy Metal's favor. Led by a backup quarterback who had never played outside of scrimmages before tonight, who would have thought? But Danny is an outstanding field general. He has played an impeccable game. Can you break down how our quarterbacks are doing, Biff Bifferson?

Biff Bifferson: I think I know what it is now. Several years ago, at the zoo, I tried to push my wife into the crocodile exhibit. She never forgave me for that. The bitch never forgave me.

Beelzebub: Going into the fourth quarter, Danny has completed 21 of 28 passes for a completion percentage of 75.0. He has thrown five touchdowns, zero interceptions, and a whopping 311 yards. By the pro formula, he holds an astronomical quarterback rating of 150.4. He's playing the game of a lifetime, folks.

Biff Bifferson: It's not like the crocodiles hurt her.

Beelzebub: (*Clearing throat.*) To the contrary, Old Time's Whiskey Nash, who broke most of Goyle Flex's league passing records this season, has all but blown his full-ride recruitment offers from some of the biggest football schools in the nation by playing the single worst game of his career, in the championship no less. Whiskey Nash is 15 for 36 with a completion

THE ROADKILL QUARTERBACK OF HEAVY METAL HIGH

percentage of 41.7, 178 yards, zero touchdowns, five interceptions, and a pro quarterback rating of 17.8. I wouldn't be surprised if the college scouts watching him tonight end up talking to Danny after the game.

Biff Bifferson: Oh shit, we's gonna cut you!

Chapter Seventeen

On the first play of their first possession of the fourth quarter, Coach Doom called in a quarterback sneak. It was an odd play choice, but would be unexpected to the defense. Danny figured Coach Doom really wanted to rub this blowout in Old Time's face.

Before the snap, lined up behind Biggie Pie, Danny turned his head and looked at the crowd cheering him on. He looked up just in time to see a drunken werewolf who looked a lot like his father being toted away by Skeletor and two other skelecops. Danny must have made a noise because Biggie Pie snapped the ball.

Unable to stop the game, Danny tucked the ball under one arm and hoped he wouldn't fumble. His tires flung grass and mud. His engine growled and he roared ahead, plowing through the pursuing defensive players before running down more players, Vampires and Death Crusaders alike.

He drove all the way down the field and lurched to a halt after passing through the end zone. *Fuck yes*, he thought, *I've always dreamed of running for a touchdown.*

The referee threw a yellow flag down on the field. Several players, including some of Danny's teammates, had not gotten up after he scored. Evidently, when he surged through the line and plowed across the field, he'd killed a few people.

The referee ran to the fifty yard line and signaled for the head coach of each team to congregate there. He spoke with Coach Doom and Old Time's coach for a few minutes. The cheerleaders on each side attempted to ease the nervous crowd with little success. The midfield conference ended with Coach Doom exploding in a fit of fury. He dropped to the grass, flailing his arms and kicking his legs. He yelled profanities so loudly that Danny figured everyone within a mile of the stadium must have heard.

"Premature killing," the referee said, "against Heavy Metal. Obligatory sacrifice of the offending player."

About half of the fans, parents, and friends of the Death Crusaders booed. The other half cheered. Danny wondered if his imminent slaughter made them happy, or if it was the prospect of a bloody game that they cheered for.

In the cab of Danny's truck-body, the chainsaw yowled like a cat that was just stepped on. It seized control of the truck and blasted Holy Diver, singing along with its grinding steel voice.

Chapter Eighteen

In the Commentary Booth:

Biff Bifferson: You're married. Tell me, does your wife's cunt stink? I think it was the fumes. The fumes wafting from my wife's cunt made me what I am. Every night it was like sleeping beside a rotten sushi roll. No wonder I drank. *Ever hear of a douche?* That's what I'd tell her. *Ever hear of a douche?*

Beelzebub: By divorcing you, Biff Bifferson, your wife left a very big douche. Indeed, the biggest douche of all.

Biff Bifferson: Hey, where do you get off calling me a douche? Just because my head is floppy doesn't make me a douche.

Beelzebub: We've got bloodshed on the field!

Biff Bifferson: Who gives a shit about those steroid-addled, privileged adolescents anyway?

Beelzebub: On a long run that brings the score to 55-17, Danny the werewolf has gone insane! I bet the refs are calling this one back.

Biff Bifferson: You can go to Hell.

Beelzebub: Danny is rampaging across the field. Now he's run over both refs and half of the Country Vampires. He's even killing his own teammates! Folks, withhold your urge to pray as we bear witness to the biggest massacre in

Heavy Metal's history. Surely God is not around to hear your sniveling last gasp.

Biff Bifferson: Don't bring God into this.

Beelzebub: I'm trying to keep him out.

Biff Bifferson: (*Muttered.*) Fucking evangelist insect.

Beelzebub: I heard that.

Biff Bifferson: Cocksucker.

Beelzebub: Can't you see what's happening on the field? Call the skelecops! Call somebody! This is a gross violation of league rules!

Biff Bifferson: My wife took my cell phone.

Beelzebub: There's a phone on the wall, over by the door.

Biff Bifferson: Not anymore. My wife took that one too. She left me with nothin' but a toothbrush. Not even a farewell note that said *Fuck off and die, Biff Bifferson.* I would've appreciated that.

Beelzebub: Biff Bifferson, I can see the phone from here. Your wife did not steal the telephone. Now get up and call the police. Danny the Psycho's already run over most of the cheerleaders. Oh, shit! He's coming our way!

(*The commentary booth fills with blood.*)

Chapter Nineteen

Danny yelped each time the crunch of another run-over player or cheerleader jolted the truck. He racked his brain for some way to halt the insane chainsaw's hit-and-run riot, but the voice of Ronnie Dio overpowered his thoughts.

"Time to hit the dirt, kid," the chainsaw said. "Don't worry, you'll live through this."

The shriek of a blade cutting through glass accompanied Ronnie for a brief demoniac harmony before a river of blood swept Danny out of his own truck-body.

Danny hit the grass. His arms scuttled over to him and reattached themselves. He remained legless.

Despite losing the gargantuan body he'd temporarily controlled, he felt thankful to be himself again, even if he was a cripple.

From where he sat on the fiftieth yard line, Danny scanned the field and sidelines. Without legs, there was no hope of running after Skeletor and his father, but at least his father escaped the massacre.

Having slaughtered virtually every Heavy Metal cheerleader, the chainsaw-driven truck zoomed straight at the fleeing Country Vampire cheer squad. Danny thought of nothing except Barbetta. The memory of her fleshless face was like a beautiful insect squirming between the teeth of his mind.

And then he saw her. She was not dead yet.

Barbetta's belly gaped open. Even at a distance, Danny thought her coiled insides looked very surprised to see him. He swore to the metal gods. Her intestines had smiled at him! *Let me suck your liver,* he might have said, if he'd stood within hearing range. Instead, he raised his arms to the autumn sky and howled her name.

Barbetta somersaulted across the field, her beatific face

curling into her long, slender legs. During each roll, Danny forgot that her ruined midsection existed. On the upturn, it reappeared, a brutal reminder of what he'd done. Her blood sprayed across the field like a powerful sprinkler, nourishing the corpses.

She somersaulted and collapsed on top of Danny, her belly-gore warming the stubs of his legs. He moved his hands over her face. He dug into her cheeks and ran his fingers over her white teeth.

"I love you, Barbetta!"

"I love you, Danny!"

All around, people screamed. An engine's roar mocked them all. Sirens wailed in the distance. It felt good to be in love.

Barbetta stroked his hair and cooed soft words into his ears. "I am roadkill like you, Danny. I have always been just roadkill."

"What do you mean, Barbetta?"

"I have secretly always loved Dio."

Danny opened his mouth to respond when a honking at midfield tore his attention away from her. The driver-side door of his father's truck flung open and the chainsaw surfed out on a wave of blood.

The chainsaw grew larger.

It grew arms.

It grew legs.

It grew a head.

It grew fucking awesome jet-black heavy metal hair.

And it sang with the voice of the holy savior, Ronnie James Dio.

"Holy Diver!"

"What's happening, Danny? How come that chainsaw looks like Dio? And sounds like Dio?"

Danny could tell Barbetta was nervous. Hell, he was nervous too.

"Stay cool. He's a friend of mine," he said, his calm voice

and smooth choice of words a surprise even to himself.
Dio stopped in front of Danny and Barbetta.
"I've come to collect the hero," Dio said.
"You mean *me*?" Danny asked.
"Yes, Danny, you're a hero now. You're the hero you've always dreamed of becoming. Congratulations. Do you want to claim your prize?"
"Do I win the girl of my dreams?"
"You already have me," Barbetta said, kissing him on the cheek.
"No, Danny," Dio said, ignoring Barbetta. "You get to spend eternity with me. In my dark, damp castle. I've got a library, a bar, a full recording studio. What do you say?"
"Just you and me, Ronnie?"
"Just you and me, champ."
"Can I bring Barbetta along?"
"Sorry, I'm afraid heroes must walk the hero's road alone."
Danny turned to Barbetta. She had tears in her eyes. "I understand, Danny. It's okay. You don't have to explain. Go be as awesome as you are. Just remember that I love you."
Before Danny could kiss Barbetta goodbye, Dio scooped him into his arms and walked away.
"Goodbye, Barbetta. I'll always love you," Danny called, peering over Dio's shoulder.
"Give it a rest, kid. The girl is dead."
The sirens were close now. Dio strode faster across the bloody grass. Danny stared slack-jawed into the face of his hero.
Dio loaded Danny into the passenger seat and hurried around to the driver's side.
"Buckle up," Dio said.
Danny buckled up.
The first cop cars pulled into Heavy Metal High's parking lot as Dio started the engine, turned the stereo up real loud, and the truck floated up into the sky.
They sang Holy Diver all the way into the clouds.

Epilogue

Danny turns to Dio and says "I mean, what the hell is Holy Diver about anyway?"

They have just watched the Holy Diver music video for the 1,829th time. It used to be Danny's favorite music video of all time. Now, it makes no fucking sense to Danny. He feels very awkward sitting in the dungeon of this dark, damp castle, watching this music video on repeat. He regrets becoming a hero and getting to spend eternity with the legend. Hanging out with Dio is not as cool as Danny thought it would be.

"Look Ronnie," Danny says, "Holy Diver is awesome and all, but don't you have anything else in this dark, damp castle? Like steampunk seahorses or ghosts that poop or . . . dragons?"

Dio flashes the horns. "Oh, I got dragons. But did you see this video?"

They watch Holy Diver.
Again.
And again.
And again.

The Destroyed Room

SLOTH IN THE CITY

Simon and Celia are biking home from a dinner party on a smoky orange night in August.

A sloth falls out of a tree in front of Celia's bike. The brakes of Celia's bike have been worn down to nothing. Plus, she is drunk. She crashes into the sloth and flips over the handlebars. She rolls in a frenzy of limbs for several yards on the plastic grass that replaced streets and sidewalks last February.

Simon leaps off his bike. He kicks the sloth in the back. The animal screams. Its eyes are gone. It reaches a clawed hand toward Simon, mewling for help. Simon kicks the animal in the face, not because he wants to hurt it. It will die soon anyway.

The sloth's head splits away from its body and rolls in front of a cyclist on the green artificial speedway. The cyclist gives Simon the middle finger. Simon raises his hands in apology, then turns back to the sloth. Nose-shaped beetles are digging into its neck.

"What the fuck," Celia says. She stands beside him now. He meant to help her up, to kiss her wounds and make her feel better, but the sick animal prevented him from going to her.

"Are you okay?" he says. He puts a hand on her lower back.

"I'm fine." She crouches over the sloth, evading Simon's hand. Simon can tell by her tone that she is annoyed.

"Watch out for the beetles," he says.

"I know," she says.

"I'm sorry you crashed into a sloth."

"I used to like sloths. Now that they live in the city, I think they're pretty stupid. I wish they would send them back to the jungle. It's like we're living in a fucking zoo."

"I kind of like having exotic animals around," Simon says.

"Even the air we breathe is manufactured."

"It's better than living underwater. The oceans are dying and we couldn't ride bikes down there."

"I guess it's good that automobiles were banished to the ocean, but what does it matter if they replaced all the trees with fake plastic ones? We're living in a false city."

"At least we can ride bikes and not get hit by cars."

"No, you only crash into sloths now."

"You think you'd get used to it after six months."

"Get used to it? Get used to it? Fuck you, Simon. I will not buy into the apathy machine. Fuck you."

"You're drunk. You shouldn't have drank tonight. If our baby has fetal alcohol syndrome, I will never forgive you."

"I thought you wanted a freak."

"Can we go home?"

"Admit that the world is a cold dead place."

"The world is a cold dead place."

"You didn't say it with feeling."

"Because I'm so cold and dead that I feel nothing. Can we go home now?"

Celia crosses her arms across her chest. "Fine. Will you read me a bedtime story?"

"Yes. What do you want me to read to you?"

"Anything. I don't care."

Simon picks up his bike and stares at the decapitated sloth. The beetles move around inside its belly, making the sloth look pregnant.

"I'm sorry you crashed into a sloth."

"You said that already."

"What do you want me to read to you?"

"Gah, you decide."

"Penguin Island?"

"You decide," Celia says, as they pedal into the fractured bloom of a late summer night.

TINY ELEPHANTS UNDERFOOT

Simon and Celia lock their bikes to a light post. They stand outside the door of their apartment, their fingers clasped loosely together. They hear the footfall and trumpeting of a miniature stampede within.

"Elephants again," Simon says.

"Impossible. I sprayed elephanticide this morning."

"The elephants are transcending our poisons. They are elementally evolving," Simon says in a monotone voice, but meaning it as a joke.

"This is serious, Simon," Celia says.

"It's just an infestation."

"They'll destroy everything we own."

Simon shrugs. "I don't like anything I own anyway."

"I think I'll kill them this time. I really think I'll kill them."

"We are beyond peaceful negotiations. We are beyond poison. We must squash the elephants beneath our shoes. We must boil their children in hot water spiced with cloves. We must be ruthless in the face of the intruder."

Celia unlocks the door and pushes it open. They stand side by side, staring into the darkness. Simon flips on a light. Tiny white elephants parade in a single-file line that spirals inward and outward like a vortex of pestilential cuteness.

Simon lets go of Celia's hand. He steps toward the parade of tiny elephants.

"Please don't kill them," Celia says.

"I thought you wanted them dead."

"I was just mad. I didn't mean it for real. They're only elephants. They don't know any better. Look how tiny they are."

"If we don't make a stand now, they'll never leave us

alone. They'll run us out of our own fucking home."

Celia is crying now.

"There's got to be another solution," she says.

"We've tried everything. There's no other solution."

"Can't we wait until morning?"

"And let the elephants shit all over the floor and keep us up all night with their trunk music, just to kill them in the morning?"

Celia nods.

Simon looks at the tiny elephants. The tiny elephants are very cute. A while ago, Simon would have liked to keep one as a pet, but he hates them now. Celia hates them too. It makes them sad to hate tiny elephants because they used to love tiny elephants, before tiny elephants were imported to the city and infested their apartment. Simon hates the government for making him hate tiny elephants.

Simon looks away from the tiny elephants. He massages the right side of his face. He has a minor toothache. "Let's go to bed. The elephants have until morning to pack their bags."

"Do you hear that?" Celia says to the elephants. "You have until morning. Then your death bell rings."

Unlike rats, tiny elephants are not afraid of humans. They do not scramble for the dark when lights come on. They are festive creatures and might be pleasant to have around, if only they did not congregate by the hundreds or thousands and make noise all night, for tiny elephants are nocturnal.

"Still want a bedtime story?" Simon says.

Celia slips her arms around him, saying, "Yes please."

They hold each other close, and in holding each other dissolve the sandpaper feelings that rubbed them raw earlier in the day, when they argued about money. They say that money is shit, but they are in debt, accumulating more debt, and learned two weeks ago that Celia is pregnant.

"I love you," Simon says.

"I know."

"You shouldn't have drank tonight."

Celia buries her face in his chest and sighs. "Are you sure you still want to start a family with me?"

"Of course I'm sure. Are you sure?"

"Of course."

Simon kisses her forehead. She pulls away from him, kicks off her laceless red shoes, and tiptoes across the apartment, careful not to squash any elephants. She climbs into bed.

Simon unties his shoes and throws them across the room. He shuffles into the bathroom, where the elephants have unwound the entire roll of toilet paper.

Simon decides to leave the toilet paper alone. Celia usually wakes up before him. He wants her to see the toilet paper and get mad at the elephants for being messy and wasteful. Then they can kill the elephants together. Maybe they will eat one. He wonders what tiny elephants taste like. He thinks that maybe he should be more concerned about the baby and less concerned about the taste of tiny elephants.

He opens the medicine cabinet and picks up his toothbrush. He squeezes a cashew-sized glob of glittering blue paste onto the frayed bristles, closes the medicine cabinet, and sticks the brush into his mouth without wetting the bristles. He stands in the bathroom doorway. While brushing he says, "Will I make a good father?"

Celia lies facedown in the pillows. The sunflower-patterned sheet is pulled up to her waist. She has taken off her shirt. Her back is a pale honeydew rind, bereft of distinguishing marks, like a desert without cacti or rocks. Her breathing is slow and heavy. She has fallen asleep.

Simon spits toothpaste foam into the sink and rinses his mouth. He swallows two aspirin for the minor toothache.

He crawls into bed after turning off all the lights except the bedside lamp. He gets under the sheet and picks up the book on the nightstand. It is a copy of The Little Prince in the original French. Although he understands almost none of it, Simon begins reading aloud from the book.

After a while, he closes the book and turns off the lamp. He curls around Celia's sleeping form, wondering if fetuses get lonely, or if loneliness only comes on after the body grows larger than a crumb.

First Light

Simon dreams that he and Celia are stapling bacon to the cardboard walls of a cathedral without doors or windows. They have coated the entire exterior of the cathedral in bacon when a yellow crow falls of out the sky and begs them, as its dying wish, to go inside the cathedral and sit very quietly. "But how can we go inside if there are no windows or doors?" Celia asks the yellow crow, who weeps profusely for it has been shot through the heart. "Ask forgiveness," the crow says, then Simon wakes up. It is an unsettling dream, not the least because he and Celia do not eat bacon, nor any other meat.

She has turned away from him in her sleep. They each take up one side of the bed, leaving the middle cold. They used to joke that they became one person as they slept. They used to sleep closer together. Now they sleep far apart, while tiny elephants cuddle on the floor around their bed.

He slides across the void of bed to spoon her. She stirs a little, pushing into him, murmuring, "Good morning."

"Did you have good dreams?"

"A sad one. We were in a funeral home, trying to swallow green pills because we had died and one of us was being forced to go away. The green pills were supposed to make us inseparable, but the pills were as large as ostrich eggs. We couldn't choke them down. It made me sad. Did you have a good dream?"

"We were outside a cathedral, doing something with bacon. I forget what."

He never remembers his dreams for long.

He moves his left hand over her hip, up the side of her body, across her chest, and down her belly.

Her belly, where the baby is.

"What the fuck," he says. "The blanket is squeezing my hand."

He throws the blankets off. Three powder blue strings protrude from Celia's bellybutton. They are as thin and transparent as fishing line.

The strings go taut.

He waves his hands back and forth. His hand passes through the strings without getting tangled or affecting them in any way, as if they possess no physical substance, like holograms. But when he makes to grab them, closing his hand into a fist, the strings feel solid in his grip. They feel cold and rubbery, like mozzarella cheese.

"What's wrong?" Celia says.

He looks at her face. The strings jutting from her belly are not the only strings. Strings come out of her hands, shoulders, feet, face.

"What's happened to you?" he says.

"Nothing," she says, wearing a panicked facial expression. "What's wrong with you?"

As she speaks, her strings move in sync with her words and gestures. Celia and the strings act in such accordance that Simon cannot tell whether she is controlling them or they are controlling her.

"There are strings coming out of you," he says. "Strings in your hands, feet, face . . . even strings coming from your belly. You must see them."

"What the fuck are you talking about? Is this a joke?"

Simon puts his hands on her shoulders and looks her straight in the eye so she knows he is serious. He speaks in a level voice. "This is not a joke. There are strings coming out of you. I don't know why you can't see them, but they're there."

She shakes her head and laughs. "I always knew you were a little crazy, but strings? Really, Simon?"

As she speaks, her body shifts like a marionette controlled by a trembling puppeteer. He imagines the strings weaving through her guts and muscles. He cannot touch her after thinking this. The strings repulse him. It is as if she is infected with a dangerous parasite. Despite his revulsion, he feels compelled to save her from these strings that are invisible to her.

"Let me cut your strings," he says, averting his eyes.

"I'm going back to bed." Celia turns her back to him and lays down. She pulls the blankets over her head. Her blue strings cut right through the blanket.

Simon tries to stay calm. He doesn't want to freak out. He feels irritated with Celia. He knows that it's irrational and that he had better stop before things escalate into a fight, but he cannot help thinking that it is her fault for not seeing the strings.

"Hold me," she says, in a half-asleep stupor.

Simon gets under the covers, but he cannot touch her.

"Let me cut your strings," he says.

"Go for it," she says.

"Do you want me to cut them with scissors, or just use my hands?"

"I don't care. Do what you feel like."

"Which do you prefer?"

"Dammit, Simon."

"Well which?"

"Hands. I don't know."

"OK, let me know if it hurts."

He reaches for the belly strings first because they are the smallest, but Celia is lying at an angle where Simon cannot reach them.

"Can you move?" he says.

She rolls over, grumbling about what an asshole he is.

Simon grabs the three belly strings in his hand and jerks on all three at once. They go slack and slide out of her belly, unbloodied, damaging her in no discernible way.

"Did you pull out my strings?" Celia says.

"Be quiet. I'm waiting to see what happens."

Nothing happens for another minute, then the strings blacken and wither. They slip out of his hand and retract into the ceiling like vines.

"Do you feel any different?" he says.

"I feel exactly the same, which is annoyed and tired."

"Sorry. I'll be done soon."

"Can't you be done now?"

"Celia, there are strings coming out of your body. I don't give a fuck if you can't see them. I want them gone. Maybe they're a new breed of insect, or probes."

Simon collects all of Celia's remaining strings in one fist, thinking again of cheese. He will pull them out all at once.

"I'm going to pull all of your strings on three, OK?" He knows telling her this will annoy her, but since it is her body they are dealing with, he thinks he should at least keep her informed. "One . . . two . . . three."

He pulls the strings.

He slides a hand under the covers as the strings go slack and dark. He strokes her lower back. "All done," he says. "Thank you for being patient with me."

Celia offers no response. Simon feels sick. "Celia? I'm sorry. Please say something," he says.

Her deteriorating strings leave a sulfuric odor in the air.

She must be really pissed to ignore him like this. He knows it is better to leave her alone. After sleeping for a few more hours she will not be mad, but Simon cannot stand letting bad feelings simmer between them, even though Celia says bad feelings are sometimes necessary.

He tries tickling her. She remains still. "Celia." Frustrated by her unresponsiveness, but also growing concerned, Simon shakes her shoulder. "Celia." She does not move. "Celia!"

THE DESTROYED ROOM

There is no question now. Celia is not breathing. Pulling out her strings has rendered her unconscious. And the baby, the baby. What about the baby?

Not knowing CPR, Simon leaps out of bed. He slips in elephant shit twice, banging his knees and elbows, before he reaches the phone on the wall.

Simon and Celia thought it would be charming to have an old-fashioned telephone. Now, as Simon struggles to pick up a dial tone on the antiquated machine, the receiver feels like a stone wheel in his hands.

Finally, the dial tone buzzes through and he punches in the emergency number. He wonders what he will say. That he has killed his wife and unborn child by ripping out the strings that tethered them to life?

"What is your emergency?"
"My pregnant wife is unconscious."
"How long has she been unconscious?"
"A few minutes I think."
"What is your location?"
"Seven-One-Seven Golden Oak Drive."
"An emergency dispatch will—"
"An emergency dispatch will what? Will be here shortly? Answer me!"

He looks at the phone, hesitant to hang up, but there is a blue string running out of his right hand, and he drops the phone.

AMBULANCE PEOPLE

Fifteen minutes later, an ambulance pulls to the curb outside the apartment. Simon opens the door. Two ambulance men dressed in gray uniforms and carrying a stretcher between them hop out of the ambulance and hurry into the apartment. One of the men has curly red hair and looks to be about Simon's age. The other man has a white handlebar mustache. The ambulance men have strings identical to Celia's strings, minus the belly strings. Simon decides to ignore the strings so the ambulance men can focus on Celia. He doesn't want to cause a scene.

The men place the stretcher next to Celia on the bed and set to work checking her vital signs.

"No pulse," the mustached one says.

"No temperature," says the one with red hair.

"Even if she's dead, she should still have a temperature."

"Well it's obviously the temperature of a dead person, so it may as well be none at all."

"Standard procedure, Dan," says the mustached one. "Temperature is protocol." He turns to Simon. "Really sorry about the attitude. He's new to the ambulance squad."

The men roll Celia onto the stretcher.

"Is she OK?" Simon asks.

"For a dead woman," Dan says.

"Oh shut up," says the mustached one. "I'm sorry to report, sir, this woman here is beyond retrieval."

"Beyond retrieval?"

"It means there's nothing we can do to bring her back."

"She's gone, chap," Dan says. "Left you for a Mister Rigor Mortis."

"What did I just tell you?" the mustached one says.

"You said she's beyond retrieval."

"Of course she is, but no! I told you to shut up. Now shut up and lift." And to Simon: "Again, I'm terribly sorry for his behavior."

The men lift the stretcher and move toward the door.

"Hold on a minute." Simon hurries in front of them, blocking their exit. "Where are you taking her?"

"Trying to keep her around for some after-hours fun, eh?" Dan says.

"Idiot!" says the mustached one. "I'll be back in a moment to discuss the paperwork."

"Paperwork?" Simon says.

"Death papers, funeral forms, a load of bollocks if you ask me," Dan says.

"Nobody asked you," says the mustached one.

The ambulance men push past Simon, balancing the stretcher between them. They load Celia into the back of the ambulance and hop in after her.

The emergency siren howls.

Simon thinks they are about to drive off, having practically abducted Celia from the apartment, when the mustached one hops out of the ambulance, holding a thick stack of papers in his hands. The mustached one yells something to Simon, but his words are drowned by the siren.

They go inside and the mustached one says, "Take a seat."

Simon sits at the table. The mustached one lays the stack of papers in front of him. He puts a pen in Simon's hand and says, "Sign here, please."

"Sign where?" Simon says.

"Anywhere. I just meant sign the forms. It doesn't matter where you sign, or what order you sign them in, but all these forms do have to be signed."

"What are they for?"

"Records and Information. Tax men. Telemarketers.

Local, state, and federal governments. The green forms contain information about the funeral. They certify that you trust the hospital to make all funeral arrangements. One of those forms is an Agreement of Notification. The hospital agrees to notify all immediate family members of the deceased. Were you her spouse?"

"Yes."

"The hospital will not contact your side of the family. They leave that up to you."

"OK."

"And friends. Should friends be attending the funeral, you will need to notify them in advance. Johnston Funeral Services handles all of our funeral affairs. Anyone who is not a member of the immediate family of the deceased must contact JFS and RSVP if they are to attend the funeral."

"Do I need to . . . RSVP?"

"No. Spouses are considered immediate family."

"Is there anything I can do? Anything I should be doing?"

"Sign these papers. Beyond that, you're off the hook. Call people, if you'd like. We have a grieving hotline, if you need. The hospital, or JFS on our behalf, will contact you soon with the date and time at which the funeral is to be held. I'm very sorry for your loss."

"Can I—"

"Can you hurry up signing the paperwork? Your wife is not the only person dead or dying today. We've got at least a dozen emergency stops after this one."

Simon signs the papers faster. His hand is beginning to cramp. Outside, the ambulance siren continues to wail. "I'm sorry. It's just—"

"I know. Hard. I'm sorry, again, for your loss."

After the final form is signed, the mustached one collects the stack of paperwork under his left arm. "The hospital will be in touch," he says. He salutes Simon and marches out of the apartment.

SEVEN PIECES OF ELECTRICAL TAPE, PLUS ONE DEAD ARM

After the ambulance goes, Simon finds a pair of scissors. They are left-handed scissors because Celia was left-handed. The scissors feel awkward in his right hand, but he is right-handed and prefers the awkward feeling of using left-handed scissors with his right hand to the awkward feeling of using any scissors with his left hand.

He cuts the string attached to his left hand. It hurts very badly. He screams. His left arm falls limp at his side. He drops the scissors. He can no longer move his left arm.

Simon curls up in a little ball on the floor. He screams into the Persian rug. The rug is stained and smeared with elephant shit. He does not care. He is in severe pain. His left arm is immobile. He has killed Celia. He has killed their unborn child. He feels destroyed. Worse, he feels guilty.

Simon picks up the scissors in his right hand. He will kill himself.

He realizes that he cannot cut the string attached to his right hand if he is holding the scissors in his right hand. He can cut all the other strings if he wants, but he fears that if he cuts all the strings except the string attached to his right hand, his spirit or whatever will be absorbed by his right arm and he will live the rest of his days as a right arm. Simon does not want to live the rest of his days as a right arm.

Out of frustration and a sense that he has reached his grieving limit, he throws the scissors against the wall.

Unlike Celia's strings, his severed string does not disintegrate or retract into the ceiling. It floats about a foot above his head.

He gets up off the floor. He has resolved to make something work. He finds some thread and needle in a drawer. He will sew his broken string back to his left hand. No he won't. He cannot thread the needle with only one hand. He does not possess that skill.

In the same drawer where he found the thread and needle, he finds a roll of electrical tape. He peels the tape back and clenches it between his teeth. He holds the tape roll in his right hand, unwinding it in a slow and cautious manner. When his arm can reach no further, he drops the tape roll and unsticks the tape from his teeth and lips.

He sticks one tape end against the back of a chair, retrieves the scissors from where they landed, and cuts off the other end. Simon repeats this six more times. It is a tedious process but eventually he has seven pieces of electrical tape that are as long as his arm.

He grabs the severed end of his string and encounters another dilemma. He cannot hold the string in place and also tape the string with only his right hand, and no matter how he strains his neck, his mouth is too far away from his left hand to perform either task.

Simon feels doomed. Today's events have distorted his mind. In his sadness and confusion, he feels bad about wasting electrical tape. He does not want the seven pieces of electrical tape to go to waste, so he tapes his left arm to his side. At least then he can pretend that he is not using his left arm by choice. It is much better to choose what you do, even if you hate doing it.

Simon sits down on the rug, still indifferent to the elephant shit. Celia will never live here again. Her organs will be passed on to other people. Her body will be donated to science. Should I move out of the apartment or keep on by myself, he wonders. The news of her death will destroy everyone.

FIRST FEW DESPERATE HOURS

On the morning of the funeral, Simon wakes up and puts on a pot of coffee. He lays two slices of whole wheat bread in the toaster oven.

He dresses in his grandfather's grey suit. He would wear something black, but he doesn't own anything black, nor any other suits. The left arm of the suit jacket hangs limp and hollow at his side.

In the bathroom, he brushes his teeth and combs his hair. He stares into the mirror above the sink while he does these things. He does not really see himself in the mirror. He only sees his strings.

The toast is burning. He can smell it. Celia's funeral is in three hours, but at the moment, burnt toast is his reality. I am expected to cry, he thinks.

In the kitchen, he turns off the toaster oven. He slides the charred toast onto a green plate, careful not to scorch his fingers. He pours a cup of coffee and sits down at the table with his black toast.

The toast crumbles like ashen logs in his mouth.

The coffee burns his tongue.

Company might be nice. He'd even welcome the tiny elephants, but the tiny elephants are gone. They sleep in the walls in the day.

He shuffles around the apartment, terrified that he will fail to occupy the hours remaining before the funeral. He wipes crumbs from the corners of his mouth and stares at the books on the shelves, anything to avoid looking at his strings.

He takes down Keats' Complete Poems.

Keats was Celia's favorite poet.

He sits down again and opens the book to a page

marked by a coupon for dog food. The coupon must have been there since before Ferdinand and Fernando died. That was what? Three, four years ago?

The dogs were born of the same litter, and they died by the same rifle, fired by the same neighbor on the same day. Said the dogs threatened his goats. Simon and Celia loved their tent cabin, tucked away in the forest on the coast north of the city, but they decided to move after the death of Ferdinand and Fernando. Maybe they would have stayed on if only one of the dogs had died, or even both, if a mountain lion or bear killed them instead. Maybe, if they stayed, Simon would have never seen the strings. He folds the dog food coupon into his breast pocket and tells himself to forget the maybes.

The pages are blank because this is a talking book. In order to be read, the book must be wound like a music box.

After he winds the book, the pages melt, then rise and fold together in the shape of a human head. The visage is that of the dead poet. The paper Keats opens his mouth and begins reading from Part Two of Hyperion. Simon is not surprised that Celia kept this page marked for so long. Hyperion was her favorite poem. Face to face with the talking paper head, Simon has to turn away. Keats' breath smells of mildew and rust, probably due to water damage. The poet's croaking voice emanates from trembling, yellowed lips:

Just as the self-same beat of Time's wide wings,
Hyperion slid into the rustled air
And Saturn gained with Thea that sad place
Where Cybele and the bruised Titans mourned.
It was a den where no insulting light
Could glimmer on their tears; where their own groans
They felt, but heard not, for the solid roar
Of thunderous waterfalls and torrents hoarse, torrents hoarse—

THE DESTROYED ROOM

The book spits up blood. A major problem with talking books is that as they get older, they assume the infirmities their human creators possessed in life. Celia's copy of Keats' Complete Poems has grown tubercular. Simon wipes the blood off the lips. It feels like blood, but when he looks at his fingers, he sees liquid words. He rubs his fingers together, smearing the words together into a blob. He shakes the book. It sputters and fast-forwards through a few lines before continuing in its normal mechanical voice:

Forehead to forehead held their monstrous horns;
And thus in thousand hugest fantasies
Made a fit roofing to this nest of woe.
Instead of thrones, hard flint they sat upon,

The book spits up blood again.

Some chained in torture, and some wandering.
Dungeoned in opaque element, to keep
Their clenched teeth still clenched, and all their limbs
Locked up like veins of metal, cramped and screwed;
Without a motion, save of their big hearts
Heaving in pain, and horribly convulsedconvulsedconvulsed
convulsed convulsedconvulsedconvulsed—

Simon rips Keats' paper head out of the book. He tears the head apart in his right hand. He wanted nothing more than to hear these words that filled Celia's heart and mind and spirit like balloon animals, but the book is a malfunctioning piece of shit.

As the words leak out of the destroyed paper head, tiny blue strings, so nearly invisible that he failed to notice them before, blacken and fall away from the book.

CATERPILLAR BUS

Simon prepares to leave the apartment for the funeral. He does not care that he will arrive early. He cannot remain where he is. He simply cannot stand his own company in this space of so many memories. He cannot stand knowing that the book was alive. It was Celia's favorite and he killed it. He loosens his tie. Maybe he's just anxious about the funeral.

On his way out, he slams the door on a hideous noise.

He spins around.

A tiny elephant's trunk has been crushed in the door.

He was not prepared for that.

Hands shaking, he fumbles with the door key. He finally manages to turn the key in the bottom lock. He opens the door.

The tiny elephant's trunk has been severed completely. The tiny elephant lies on its side, bleeding to death, choking.

Simon takes off his suit jacket and wraps the tiny elephant in it. He failed to notice the creature on his way out. It must have tried to follow or squeeze out behind him. He sits on the floor in the doorway, cradling the elephant in his right arm.

The elephant dies. Its strings dissolve, floating off in wispy flakes. Simon holds his breath so as not to breathe them in.

He shakes the elephant out of the jacket, onto the floor. Blood has seeped through the jacket. Blood stains his pants and shirt.

He moves the elephant's severed trunk with his foot until the elephant and the severed trunk lie side by side. They look like two sleeping creatures. If not for all the blood, they would look peaceful.

Feeling disgraceful, Simon puts on his jacket and leaves the apartment, careful not to smash any elephants on his way out.

He is concerned about riding a bicycle with only one arm. Even if he removes the electrical tape, his left arm will not function, so he leaves the arm taped, the left sleeve of the grey and bloody jacket unfilled.

When the hospital called with the date and time of the funeral, they also gave him directions and an address. He takes the piece of paper he'd written these things on out of his pocket. He looks it over. Although the hospital is only three miles away, Simon has never visited the city sector where it is located.

He gets on his bike. He pedals down the street, right hand on the handlebars and then no hands. This is the first time he has left the apartment since Celia's death. He realizes how hard this is going to be.

He failed to consider how seeing strings might affect his getting around. Biking one-armed isn't even the hard part. There are so many things alive in the world, so many strings crossing other strings. He feels as if he is riding into a citywide spider web. The blue strings of people, birds, sloths, elephants, badgers, and other city dwellers thread the streets and sky, connecting the invisible dots of the psychogeographic landscape that maps every impulse, routine, pressure, and pleasure of the city's circuitry.

An eagle swoops down. It is tiger-eyed, its talons outstretched. A tiny elephant stumbles into Simon's path. The eagle's strings coil around the elephant's strings as the eagle swoops down. Unable to swerve out of the way, Simon crashes his bike out of fear that his strings will crisscross those of the predator and its prey.

He sits up, strawberry patches for elbows and knees, as the eagle lifts the elephant toward the sun.

He must hurry to the funeral. He is no longer due to

arrive early. He picks up his bicycle and wheels it along beside him.

He steps in a gutter full of water and says, "Fucking hell."

He contemplates running into the street and pulling all his strings. Why wait to die. He figures he'd better wait until after the funeral. Touching Celia's coffin is the closest he'll ever get to holding her again, unless there's a Heaven and they both get to go there. Maybe they'll reincarnate as slugs. They will rejoice, reliving the love and happiness of their human days, only slimier.

A caterpillar bus turns onto the street. Simon has always been afraid of caterpillar buses. He has never been good at riding with other people, let alone a few dozen strangers all at once.

The conductor of the caterpillar bus yells at the passengers to slow down. "Where you heading?" he calls to Simon.

"I'm going to the funeral home," Simon says.

A few people shout for him to go away. The conductor tells them to knock it off. He turns to Simon. "That's a steep climb. What are you willing to pay?"

Simon reaches into his pocket for his wallet. He removes a wad of bills from his wallet and hands the bills to the conductor, feeling glad that he always carries his money around despite the many times he has been called old-fashioned for doing so. Unfortunately, he is now totally broke. The conductor counts the money and nods. "Climb aboard," he says.

Climbing is not actually necessary to board the caterpillar bus. It is a huge metal caterpillar with bicycles instead of legs. The passengers pedal to operate a hydrogen engine located in the head. When the caterpillar bus moves fast enough, the hydrogen engine forms bubbles. The bubbles float out of a brass smoking pipe welded between the caterpillar's lips.

Simon secures his bike just behind the caterpillar's head, upon which the conductor sits behind an enormous steering wheel. The conductor shouts for everyone to pedal. Simon and the rest of the passengers begin to pedal. Since there are not many passengers, the caterpillar bus is very wobbly, like it is missing most of its legs.

As they pick up speed, bubbles float out of the caterpillar's brass pipe, but the momentum quickly dies. There are not enough passengers to propel the caterpillar bus to go any faster. At this slow pace, Simon would almost be better off walking. Fortunately, the conductor does all the steering.

"We were moving along quite well before you came along," a person behind him shouts.

"That funeral better be for someone important," shouts another.

"It's for my wife," Simon shouts.

"He says it's for his wife!"

"His wife? He's riding a bicycle to his wife's funeral?"

"What a disgrace!"

"An imbecile."

"He's a slow rider too."

"Making us ride all the way up the damned mountain."

"And filthy. Take a look at his clothes."

"I'd looked forward to this ride."

"The funeral boy has ruined it for us all."

"A disgrace."

The passengers of the caterpillar bus continue to berate him as they teeter out of the city and through a forest of plastic trees. They ascend a narrow mountain road so steep that Simon must hook his chin over his handlebars to prevent from falling backwards.

When the caterpillar bus halts to let him off, Simon realizes that all the other passengers have tumbled off their bikes. The caterpillar bus must contain reserves of hydrogen or some other fuel source. Simon thinks this is illegal but says nothing. He could never have propelled the bus up the mountain by himself.

"It's not much further," the conductor says.

Simon detaches his bike from the caterpillar bus and thanks the man. He continues on foot, thankful that the road has leveled off, as the caterpillar bus turns around and begins its slow crawl down the mountain.

THE FUNERAL

A sign on the side of the road proclaims WELCOME TO JOHNSTON FUNERAL SERVICES. An empty parking lot overtaken by plastic blackberry bushes comes into view. Beyond the field of bushes, a glass dome sparkles in the hot afternoon sun. Skinny blue strings protrude from the glass walls. The strings sway in a light breeze. Simon follows them with his eyes, but the sunlight obscures their endpoints. For all he knows, they continue into outer space, and perhaps even further.

Simon locks his bike to a FUNERAL PARKING ONLY sign and approaches the glass dome.

A path cut in the blackberry bushes leads up to the dome. The path is overgrown. He is cut by plastic thorns.

Simon remembers when he and Celia went to Newport Beach and the same jellyfish stung them both. At the memory, his mouth creases into a smile, sadness filling him like sand. That was their first vacation together. The weather was miserable, the motel had cockroaches and moldy sheets, and they got stung by a jellyfish, yet they had the most beautiful time together.

He approaches the doorway cut into the glass dome. The dome seems fancy for a funeral home. The strings rising through it belong to trees. Real trees.

Amidst the tree strings, there are smaller strings attached to the fruit that hang from branches. Simon has not seen a fruit tree in almost a full year. He doesn't recognize the purplish fruit growing on the trees. He thinks they are plums.

He follows a cluster of larger strings down to the person they are attached to. She is a skeletal old woman swathed in vibrant greens, yellows, and reds. She is not frightening to look at, nor is she pretty.

"Excuse me," he says, rapping lightly on the glass.

The old woman looks up. Her lips have been eaten away by something black. Simon casts his eyes to his shoes. "I'm here for the funeral."

The pressure behind his face swells. He closes his eyes, afraid his eyeballs will pop out. His knees buckle. He steps inside the glass dome and leans against the wall for support.

The old woman limps toward him. She stops to pick some fruit off of a tree. When she gets close enough, she hands him a piece of fruit.

"What is it?" says Simon.

"Pluot."

"Thank you."

"It's good."

Simon looks at the smooth-fleshed, purple fruit. It fits perfectly in his right palm. As he holds the fruit, the blue string coiled around the stem disintegrates.

"Eat it," the old woman says. "It's good."

Simon takes a bite. He chews slowly. He doesn't know why he received this gift. He only accepted it to be kind. He has never tasted a sweeter, juicier pluot.

"The ceremony is about to begin," the old woman says. "You can follow me over there."

"Are you the groundskeeper?"

"I'm the accountant."

"The accountant?"

"I settle the books of the dead. These days I bury the bodies and keep JFS running, what with budget cuts and layoffs they've even released the gardener, but officially, I'm just the accountant."

"Is anyone else here . . . for Celia?" Simon asks.

"No one yet."

"Maybe they're running late," Simon says.

"Did you expect anyone?"

"No one in particular."

THE DESTROYED ROOM

The accountant shakes her head sadly. "No one ever shows up late to these."

The mustached one said the hospital would send a notice of death to everyone in Celia's immediate family. However, Celia had been estranged from her family since before Simon met her. He has never even met her parents.

He intended to call his and Celia's friends, and also his family.

He failed to call anyone.

The accountant walks past him out of the glass dome and says, "Follow me."

"Where are we going?" Simon says.

He cannot feels his limbs. He thinks he must be going into shock. He's out of breath. He cannot breathe. He stares up at the glass dome pixilated by tears. A plane screams high above.

"We don't do funerals in the garden. Come around to the parlor."

"OK," Simon says.

The accountant bustles away. Although she is barefoot, she walks at a fast clip. The patchwork fabric of her dress billows around her like a carnival tilt-a-whirl. Simon has to jog to stay by her side.

The accountant's presence calms him a little bit, but uncertainty and shame gnaw at him. Uncertainty about the nature and regiment of funeral affairs. Shame over the absence of mourners, the absence of flowers. He failed to bring flowers.

"Do people still bring flowers to funerals?" he asks. "I know from reading articles that it used to be traditional, but what's the tradition now? I've never been to a funeral. I don't know what's expected. Are flowers normal? Am I doing something wrong?"

The accountant tilts her head and stares at him. Her eyes are cold and mean. Her blackened maw cracks into a smile.

They walk along a trail of stones that curves around

the glass dome and zigzags through the fields beyond up to a trailer overtaken by flowering vines. The vines are blue and Simon initially mistakes them for strings.

"These vines are fake," he says. He knows this because the vines do not possess strings. He has learned that living things have strings attached.

"No, they're not," the accountant says.

The accountant pulls a set of keys from beneath her dress and unlocks the door of the trailer. They go inside.

The trailer is the standard classroom type. Cheap variegated carpet on the floors, burlap curtains over the windows, pastel butcher paper stapled to the walls to hide the structural cheerlessness, and a sputtering heating/cooling unit in the corner. Simon has not set foot in one of these since his school days. Rows of black foldout chairs fill most of the room. In front, a podium and a coffin rest on a plywood riser.

"Take a seat," the accountant says, approaching the podium.

"Is Celia in the coffin," Simon says.

"It's her funeral, isn't it?" The accountant does not pause or turn around to respond.

"Can I look?"

"Look later."

Simon chooses a seat in the first row, center. He pictures every chair in the trailer occupied, except for those in the front row because the other funeral attendees, in awe of the depth of his grief, have left the front row empty. People stand in the back, but nobody dares sit in the front row with Simon. He can almost hear the people whisper, "That man loved her," and "She loved that man," and "True love found them," and "Even now, I long for what they had," and "It's always like this."

Simon turns in his seat, first caught in his daydream and then by the empty chairs. Family and friends are not here.

The accountant clears her throat.
He faces her.
"Celia Conk is survived by her husband, Simon Conk."
He clenches his right hand in his lap.
"The records of her birth and early life are contradictory and incomplete, and are therefore unworthy of repeating. In recent years, she graduated from Gramercy College with a Bachelors of Science in Ornithology. She was employed by the St. George Free Zoo from the month of her graduation until April of this year. At the time of her death, Celia Conk was $1,916 in debt. She had not made a payment toward nullifying her debt since her termination from St. George. Her life was presumably a happy one, albeit short."

The accountant sighs. She looks bored.
"Is that all?" Simon asks.
"Unless you have something to add."

Simon rises and approaches the coffin. He kneels beside it, presses his right hand against the lacquered lid about where he estimates Celia's face to be, and bows his head. He has never been to a funeral so maybe this is how all of them go, but it feels wrong to him. There must be something he can say.

Nothing rises. Maybe silence is best. No reason to fill her coffin with words. Words don't help the dead.

"Do you have anything more to add?" the accountant says.

Simon opens his eyes and looks at the accountant. He realizes that his face is wet. "That is all," he says.

"Since it's only the two of us, do you mind if we discuss payment here," the accountant says.

"Payment?"
"Funerals aren't free, you know."
"Is there somewhere else we can go to discuss payment? I mean—" he gestures to the coffin.

"I'm afraid I shouldn't have suggested that we have

another option. My office is all the way across the property and I've got to bury yours and prepare the next body before my three o'clock appointment arrives. There's really no time."

The next body. Three o'clock appointment. These are the terms of death. Simon hates this old woman who calls herself the accountant.

She takes a black binder from the podium and steps off the plywood riser, comes and sits next to him. She opens the binder across her lap and clicks her tongue against her teeth, like a teacher attempting to show a failing student what they're doing wrong.

"Total cost is $1,916."

"How can it be that much? You hardly did anything."

"The cost of a basic funeral is the debt owed by the deceased at the time of death. Had your wife owed nothing, her funeral would be free."

"Nobody said anything about payment."

"It's in the agreement that you signed. Ignorance does not absolve responsibility."

"Will Celia's debt be cleared, or is this additional?"

"It's additional."

"Can I pay in installments?"

"There's a monthly plan, but I warn you, the interest is steep."

"Fine."

"How much would you like to pay now?"

"Can you mail the bill? I'm afraid there's nothing I can do today."

The accountant studies his suit. She has a look on her face that says she's registering the blood and sweat and mud for the first time. She seems to spend a long time studying the flopping sleeve of his suit jacket.

"You've had a bad time of this," she says. She shuts the binder and looks at her wristwatch. "If we hurry, I suppose there's time to run over to my office."

"Is there more to discuss?"

"The monthly installment form is in my office. If you take it with you, it'll save me a stamp."

"If it means that much."

"It does."

The accountant springs up from the foldout chair, knocking it to the ground as she charges for the door.

Simon picks up the fallen chair and hurries after her. He has to sprint to keep up. He feels awkward and unbalanced, hustling down the stone path with one arm taped to his side.

About a hundred yards behind the trailer, they come upon another trailer. The accountant goes inside and Simon follows. Except for a white desk, three foldout chairs, and several rusting file cabinets, the trailer is bare.

"Sit down," the accountant says.

Simon collapses in a chair and rests his forehead on the edge of the desk. He is breathless. His side aches.

The accountant opens a file cabinet and removes a green document. She sits across the desk from him, studying the document. "You have twelve months from today to pay for all funeral expenses, including interest," she says, sliding the form across the desk.

Simon sits up. He creases the form down the middle and stuffs it into his inner breast pocket.

"Anything else?"

"Give me your hand," the accountant says.

Simon places his right hand palm-up on the desk.

"The other hand."

"I can't. I taped my left arm to my side."

"Why would you do such a thing?"

"It was acting up."

"Let me look at it. Maybe I can help."

"It won't move."

The accountant comes around the desk and stops behind Simon. She puts her hands on his shoulders. "Let me look."

Simon shrugs. He is too confused to resist. Plus, maybe if he lets the accountant look at his arm, she'll take pity and reduce the amount owed for the funeral.

She removes his jacket and rolls up the left sleeve of his shirt. She tears off a piece of electrical tape. Simon flinches. Hair and skin come away with the tape, but the pain does not alert his left arm into action.

The accountant lifts his left arm and lays Simon's hand palm-up on the desk. She reaches above him, grabs the withered string that used to be attached to his left hand, and returns to her side of the desk. She opens a drawer, comes up with a little sewing kit, and removes a needle and blue thread. Simon is too shocked to get up and run out of the trailer.

"Be still and don't speak," the accountant says.

"But how can you—"

"I said shut up."

Simon obeys.

The accountant grips his left hand string between her teeth while she threads the needle. After the needle is threaded, she loops it in and out of the severed end of his left hand string.

She lowers the string to the center of his left palm.

"This might hurt, but it won't take long," she says.

She weaves the needle in and out of his palm. Every time the needle enters his hand, it feels like a tattoo gun being pushed too deep. But she's right, it doesn't take long.

As soon as his string is sewn back to his hand, she bites and ties the thread, and returns the thread and needle to the sewing kit.

Simon digs his fingers into his palm.

He can move his left arm again.

Although the funeral just ended, he suddenly feels very excited.

He leaps out of his chair and says, "You see them too."

He has so many questions for her.

"Get out," she says. "I have much work left to do. Your business here is done. If you have any questions about the monthly payment plan, Johnston Funeral Services has an automated telephone system."

"What about the strings? I have questions about the strings."

The accountant points at the door and shouts, "Get out."

"But—"

"I'll call the police."

Simon throws on his jacket and walks out the door. As he walks down the stone path, he hears some keys jangle behind him. He looks back without losing stride. The accountant is locking the door to her office. She must be scared or worried that he'll return. He shrugs and sticks his hands in his pockets. At least he has his left arm back, and also confirmation that he's not the only one who sees the strings. Maybe someday he'll meet others. Maybe they'll talk about it. Maybe he will tell the truth about Celia. Maybe he will not.

It is his, this secret of the strings, of how he killed Celia and their unborn child. It is his secret.

THE DESTROYED ROOM

Simon unlocks his bike from the FUNERAL PARKING ONLY sign. A parade of mourners crosses the parking lot. Some of the people are wheezing and keeling over. As Simon walks past the mourners, an old man who looks like a walrus points at Simon's bicycle and says, "How vulgar. How dreadfully vulgar." None of the mourners have bikes with them. Biking to a funeral must be an improper thing to do. Simon lowers his head and continues on, ashamed.

He arrives at the main road and stops, allowing the last stragglers of the funeral march to pass before mounting his bike. The mountain is far steeper than it seemed on the way up. He feels nervous about riding down, so he takes a few minutes to admire the view, which he failed to notice during his ascent.

From the entrance of Johnston Funeral Services, he has a view of the entire city far below. It appears small and trapped, a pit of civilization surrounded by a plastic forest that swallows the horizon. The tinfoil bristling of the trees around him is ugly. He wishes the breeze would stop.

He has never biked down a mountain this steep. He might hurt himself. Maybe physical pain will distract him from the other pain. Considering the last few days, he'd welcome a broken bone. A smashed skull would be sublime. He'd lick gray matter from his lips and taste Celia.

He will not crash, although he likes to fantasize what would happen if he did. He just wants to go home. When he gets home, he will clean the apartment, take a hot shower and sleeping pills, and sleep for twelve hours. Then he can start making plans for the rest of his life.

He repositions his hands on the handlebars and kicks off. There's no reason to pedal. He gains speed in no time at all. Every bump in the road vibrates through his entire body, his skinny bike absorbing none of the shock. The wind is deafening, like swallowing an ocean in each ear. He's moving faster than he feels comfortable moving. The wind stings his eyes and pries his mouth into a flapping smile. He's crying, from the wind and from grief, but also from exhilaration.

A dark shape rolls into the road, directly into Simon's path.

Simon cannot use his brakes. He's going too fast.

The dark shape stands and raises its hands above its head, urging Simon to stop. He can see it clearly now. The dark shape is a sloth.

He swerves to the right to dodge around the sloth while the sloth also moves to the right in a miscalculated attempt to avoid his bicycle. He tries to correct his move, but too late and too sharply. This could be fatal, he thinks.

He collides with the sloth.

The sloth acts more like a ramp than a road block, launching Simon off the side of the road.

The bike falls away from him. He is weightless and almost floating, then he's falling after the bike, toward the bottom of a gulch so far fucking down it may as well be bottomless. Oh fuck stop falling, he thinks. Oh fuck stop falling, is all he can think.

He claws at the air out of desperation.

And he grabs onto something.

And he stops falling.

He's hanging over the gulch by two of his own strings, suspended in midair. He grabbed the strings because they were the only thing he could touch. He should be dead right now. Instead, he swings in midair, hundreds of feet over fake trees and sharp rocks. The road is thirty feet away and maybe a hundred feet up.

How fast was he going and how high was he launched to soar thirty feet? He tries doing the math, but the numbers ooze like broken yolks across his mind. How possible or impossible his arrival to this point in time and space is irrelevant because he is here now, and he'll die if he doesn't get elsewhere.

No matter how hard he tries to hold on, he's going to fall. His arms will lose the strength to hold him up. His death has only been delayed. He is still going to die in the gulch. He is still going to die today.

He starts to climb. His strings are taut, betraying no sign that they're about to fall out of the sky.

He climbs fast. His muscles ache and his breathing is ragged, but he keeps moving. He fears that if he pauses to rest, he might never get going again. A short break might kill him.

After climbing for a while, he comes level to the road. Now he has two options. He can climb a bit higher, swing from his strings, and hopefully land on the road, or he can forget about the road and survival, just say fuck everything and climb as high as the strings and his body will allow. Neither option guarantees survival.

His body decides for him. It moves upward faster and faster, eating up strings at an incredible pace. He has no idea what to expect, so he expects nothing. He should be lying dead in the gulch. Or he and Celia should have had a child, grown old together, died together. They had talked about that, how when they got to be a certain age they would meet in a dream and leave their bodies behind. They said that's how they'd live forever, by running away. Now Simon is running away. It is not a dream; he's doing it alone.

He climbs faster. His limbs feel like burning matchsticks, but he does not dare stop. The air grows thin, hard to breathe.

The blue sky assumes a feathery texture. A chartreuse trembling gnaws at the edges. The sky is molting.

Strings crisscross everywhere.

Simon shudders with anticipation and exhaustion as he reaches an altitude where he can no longer breathe. He cannot go on, but he must. He must be close to breaking into outer space. He goes on. After a while, a square of darkness forms above. The strings are now so thick around him that he cannot see the sky. There are only the strings and the darkness above. The square of darkness must be the source of the strings.

Simon's strings begin to merge with all the rest, forming one massive blue stalk.

I'm never coming down again, he thinks.

Closer, the darkness reveals its substance.

The darkness is made of wood.

The blue stalk hangs from the dark square like the cord of a household appliance.

Finally, Simon pulls himself up onto the dark wooden square that floats in the sky. He can see the charred remains of walls around three sides. This was once a room. His hands are bloody leaves. The dark square has scalded his hands, but when he screams, he does not scream out of pain.

A dead, half-eaten shark lies on the wooden platform. The tail of the shark is missing. Its blackened ribs jut out from rotting folds of skin like broken cast-iron fence posts. The stalk of tangled strings vanishes into the festering, cave-like hollow of the shark's head. The strings are sprouting from the shark's brain.

The shark's mouth is clamped shut, as if it died while grinding its teeth or smiling.

He is alive, alone with the shark head in the sky.

ABOUT THE AUTHOR

Cameron Pierce is the author of *Shark Hunting in Paradise Garden*, *Ass Goblins of Auschwitz*, *Lost in Cat Brain Land* and *The Pickled Apocalypse of Pancake Island*. He has been a taxidermist's assistant, a paperboy, a shellfish farmer, and a college dropout. He grew up in southern California and lives in Portland, Oregon.

Visit him online at:
www.meatmagick.wordpress.com.

ABOUT THE ARTIST

Hauke Vagt was born in Hamburg, Germany. In 1997, he relocated to Lisbon, Portugal, where he works as a street painter and freelance illustrator.

Bizarro books

CATALOG SPRING 2011

Bizarro Books publishes under the following imprints:

www.rawdogscreamingpress.com

www.eraserheadpress.com

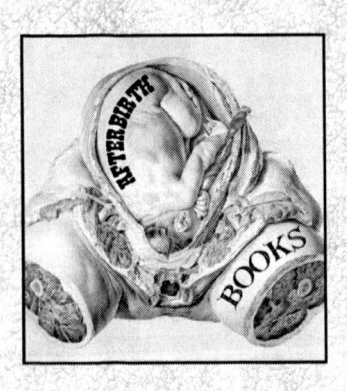

www.afterbirthbooks.com

www.swallowdownpress.com

For all your Bizarro needs visit:

WWW.BIZARROCENTRAL.COM

Introduce yourselves to the bizarro fiction genre and all of its authors with the Bizarro Starter Kit series. Each volume features short novels and short stories by ten of the leading bizarro authors, designed to give you a perfect sampling of the genre for only $10.

BB-0X1
"The Bizarro Starter Kit"
(Orange)
Featuring D. Harlan Wilson, Carlton Mellick III, Jeremy Robert Johnson, Kevin L Donihe, Gina Ranalli, Andre Duza, Vincent W. Sakowski, Steve Beard, John Edward Lawson, and Bruce Taylor. **236 pages $10**

BB-0X2
"The Bizarro Starter Kit"
(Blue)
Featuring Ray Fracalossy, Jeremy C. Shipp, Jordan Krall, Mykle Hansen, Andersen Prunty, Eckhard Gerdes, Bradley Sands, Steve Aylett, Christian TeBordo, and Tony Rauch. **244 pages $10**

BB-0X2
"The Bizarro Starter Kit"
(Purple)
Featuring Russell Edson, Athena Villaverde, David Agranoff, Matthew Revert, Andrew Goldfarb, Jeff Burk, Garrett Cook, Kris Saknussemm, Cody Goodfellow, and Cameron Pierce **264 pages $10**

BB-001 "The Kafka Effekt" D. Harlan Wilson - A collection of forty-four irreal short stories loosely written in the vein of Franz Kafka, with more than a pinch of William S. Burroughs sprinkled on top. **211 pages $14**

BB-002 "Satan Burger" Carlton Mellick III - The cult novel that put Carlton Mellick III on the map ... Six punks get jobs at a fast food restaurant owned by the devil in a city violently overpopulated by surreal alien cultures. **236 pages $14**

BB-003 "Some Things Are Better Left Unplugged" Vincent Sakwoski - Join The Man and his Nemesis, the obese tabby, for a nightmare roller coaster ride into this postmodern fantasy. **152 pages $10**

BB-004 "Shall We Gather At the Garden?" Kevin L Donihe - Donihe's Debut novel. Midgets take over the world, The Church of Lionel Richie vs. The Church of the Byrds, plant porn and more! **244 pages $14**

BB-005 "Razor Wire Pubic Hair" Carlton Mellick III - A genderless humandildo is purchased by a razor dominatrix and brought into her nightmarish world of bizarre sex and mutilation. **176 pages $11**

BB-006 "Stranger on the Loose" D. Harlan Wilson - The fiction of Wilson's 2nd collection is planted in the soil of normalcy, but what grows out of that soil is a dark, witty, otherworldly jungle... **228 pages $14**

BB-007 "The Baby Jesus Butt Plug" Carlton Mellick III - Using clones of the Baby Jesus for anal sex will be the hip sex fetish of the future. **92 pages $10**

BB-008 "Fishyfleshed" Carlton Mellick III - The world of the past is an illogical flatland lacking in dimension and color, a sick-scape of crispy squid people wandering the desert for no apparent reason. **260 pages $14**

BB-009 "Dead Bitch Army" Andre Duza - Step into a world filled with racist teenagers, cannibals, 100 warped Uncle Sams, automobiles with razor-sharp teeth, living graffiti, and a pissed-off zombie bitch out for revenge. **344 pages $16**

BB-010 "The Menstruating Mall" Carlton Mellick III - "The Breakfast Club meets Chopping Mall as directed by David Lynch." - Brian Keene **212 pages $12**

BB-011 "Angel Dust Apocalypse" Jeremy Robert Johnson - Meth-heads, man-made monsters, and murderous Neo-Nazis. "Seriously amazing short stories..." - Chuck Palahniuk, author of Fight Club **184 pages $11**

BB-012 "Ocean of Lard" Kevin L Donihe / Carlton Mellick III - A parody of those old Choose Your Own Adventure kid's books about some very odd pirates sailing on a sea made of animal fat. **176 pages $12**

BB-015 "Foop!" Chris Genoa - Strange happenings are going on at Dactyl, Inc, the world's first and only time travel tourism company.
"A surreal pie in the face!" - Christopher Moore **300 pages $14**

BB-020 "Punk Land" Carlton Mellick III - In the punk version of Heaven, the anarchist utopia is threatened by corporate fascism and only Goblin, Mortician's sperm, and a blue-mohawked female assassin named Shark Girl can stop them. **284 pages $15**

BB-021 "Pseudo-City" D. Harlan Wilson - Pseudo-City exposes what waits in the bathroom stall, under the manhole cover and in the corporate boardroom, all in a way that can only be described as mind-bogglingly irreal. **220 pages $16**

BB-023 "Sex and Death In Television Town" Carlton Mellick III - In the old west, a gang of hermaphrodite gunslingers take refuge from a demon plague in Telos: a town where its citizens have televisions instead of heads. **184 pages $12**

BB-027 "Siren Promised" Jeremy Robert Johnson & Alan M Clark - Nominated for the Bram Stoker Award. A potent mix of bad drugs, bad dreams, brutal bad guys, and surreal/incredible art by Alan M. Clark. **190 pages $13**

BB-030 "Grape City" Kevin L. Donihe - More Donihe-style comedic bizarro about a demon named Charles who is forced to work a minimum wage job on Earth after Hell goes out of business. **108 pages $10**

BB-031 "Sea of the Patchwork Cats" Carlton Mellick III - A quiet dreamlike tale set in the ashes of the human race. For Mellick enthusiasts who also adore The Twilight Zone. **112 pages $10**

BB-032 "Extinction Journals" Jeremy Robert Johnson - An uncanny voyage across a newly nuclear America where one man must confront the problems associated with loneliness, insane dieties, radiation, love, and an ever-evolving cockroach suit with a mind of its own. **104 pages $10**

BB-034 "The Greatest Fucking Moment in Sports" Kevin L. Donihe - In the tradition of the surreal anti-sitcom Get A Life comes a tale of triumph and agape love from the master of comedic bizarro. **108 pages $10**

BB-035 "The Troublesome Amputee" John Edward Lawson - Disturbing verse from a man who truly believes nothing is sacred and intends to prove it. **104 pages $9**

BB-037 "The Haunted Vagina" Carlton Mellick III - It's difficult to love a woman whose vagina is a gateway to the world of the dead. **132 pages $10**

BB-042 "Teeth and Tongue Landscape" Carlton Mellick III - On a planet made out of meat, a socially-obsessive monophobic man tries to find his place amongst the strange creatures and communities that he comes across. **110 pages $10**

BB-043 "War Slut" Carlton Mellick III - Part "1984," part "Waiting for Godot," and part action horror video game adaptation of John Carpenter's "The Thing." **116 pages $10**

BB-045 "Dr. Identity" D. Harlan Wilson - Follow the Dystopian Duo on a killing spree of epic proportions through the irreal postcapitalist city of Bliptown where time ticks sideways, artificial Bug-Eyed Monsters punish citizens for consumer-capitalist lethargy, and ultraviolence is as essential as a daily multivitamin. **208 pages $15**

BB-047 "Sausagey Santa" Carlton Mellick III - A bizarro Christmas tale featuring Santa as a piratey mutant with a body made of sausages. 124 pages $10

BB-048 "Misadventures in a Thumbnail Universe" Vincent Sakowski - Dive deep into the surreal and satirical realms of neo-classical Blender Fiction, filled with television shoes and flesh-filled skies. **120 pages $10**

BB-049 "Vacation" Jeremy C. Shipp - Blueblood Bernard Johnson leaves his boring life behind to go on The Vacation, a year-long corporate sponsored odyssey. But instead of seeing the world, Bernard is captured by terrorists, becomes a key figure in secret drug wars, and, worse, doesn't once miss his secure American Dream. **160 pages $14**

BB-053 "Ballad of a Slow Poisoner" Andrew Goldfarb Millford Mutterwurst sat down on a Tuesday to take his afternoon tea, and made the unpleasant discovery that his elbows were becoming flatter. **128 pages $10**

BB-055 "Help! A Bear is Eating Me" Mykle Hansen - The bizarro, heartwarming, magical tale of poor planning, hubris and severe blood loss... **150 pages $11**

BB-056 "Piecemeal June" Jordan Krall - A man falls in love with a living sex doll, but with love comes danger when her creator comes after her with crab-squid assassins. **90 pages $9**

BB-058 "The Overwhelming Urge" Andersen Prunty - A collection of bizarro tales by Andersen Prunty. **150 pages $11**

BB-059 "Adolf in Wonderland" Carlton Mellick III - A dreamlike adventure that takes a young descendant of Adolf Hitler's design and sends him down the rabbit hole into a world of imperfection and disorder. **180 pages $11**

BB-061 "Ultra Fuckers" Carlton Mellick III - Absurdist suburban horror about a couple who enter an upper middle class gated community but can't find their way out. **108 pages $9**

BB-062 "House of Houses" Kevin L. Donihe - An odd man wants to marry his house. Unfortunately, all of the houses in the world collapse at the same time in the Great House Holocaust. Now he must travel to House Heaven to find his departed fiancee. **172 pages $11**

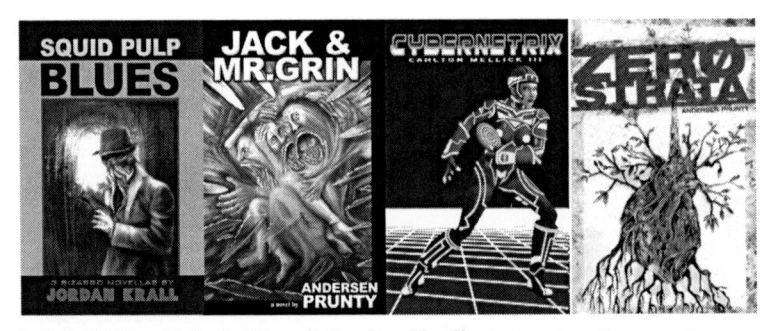

BB-064 "Squid Pulp Blues" Jordan Krall - In these three bizarro-noir novellas, the reader is thrown into a world of murderers, drugs made from squid parts, deformed gun-toting veterans, and a mischievous apocalyptic donkey. **204 pages $12**

BB-065 "Jack and Mr. Grin" Andersen Prunty - "When Mr. Grin calls you can hear a smile in his voice. Not a warm and friendly smile, but the kind that seizes your spine in fear. You don't need to pay your phone bill to hear it. That smile is in every line of Prunty's prose." - Tom Bradley. **208 pages $12**

BB-066 "Cybernetrix" Carlton Mellick III - What would you do if your normal everyday world was slowly mutating into the video game world from Tron? **212 pages $12**

BB-072 "Zerostrata" Andersen Prunty - Hansel Nothing lives in a tree house, suffers from memory loss, has a very eccentric family, and falls in love with a woman who runs naked through the woods every night. **144 pages $11**

BB-073 "The Egg Man" Carlton Mellick III - It is a world where humans reproduce like insects. Children are the property of corporations, and having an enormous ten-foot brain implanted into your skull is a grotesque sexual fetish. Mellick's industrial urban dystopia is one of his darkest and grittiest to date. **184 pages $11**

BB-074 "Shark Hunting in Paradise Garden" Cameron Pierce - A group of strange humanoid religious fanatics travel back in time to the Garden of Eden to discover it is invested with hundreds of giant flying maneating sharks. **150 pages $10**

BB-075 "Apeshit" Carlton Mellick III - Friday the 13th meets Visitor Q. Six hipster teens go to a cabin in the woods inhabited by a deformed killer. An incredibly fucked-up parody of B-horror movies with a bizarro slant. **192 pages $12**

BB-076 "Fuckers of Everything on the Crazy Shitting Planet of the Vomit At smosphere" Mykle Hansen - Three bizarro satires. Monster Cocks, Journey to the Center of Agnes Cuddlebottom, and Crazy Shitting Planet. **228 pages $12**

BB-077 "The Kissing Bug" Daniel Scott Buck - In the tradition of Roald Dahl, Tim Burton, and Edward Gorey, comes this bizarro anti-war children's story about a bohemian conenose kissing bug who falls in love with a human woman. **116 pages $10**

BB-078 "MachoPoni" Lotus Rose - It's My Little Pony... *Bizarro* style! A long time ago Poniworld was split in two. On one side of the Jagged Line is the Pastel Kingdom, a magical land of music, parties, and positivity. On the other side of the Jagged Line is Dark Kingdom inhabited by an army of undead ponies. **148 pages $11**

BB-079 "The Faggiest Vampire" Carlton Mellick III - A Roald Dahl-esque children's story about two faggy vampires who partake in a mustache competition to find out which one is truly the faggiest. **104 pages $10**

BB-080 "Sky Tongues" Gina Ranalli - The autobiography of Sky Tongues, the biracial hermaphrodite actress with tongues for fingers. Follow her strange life story as she rises from freak to fame. **204 pages $12**

BB-081 "Washer Mouth" Kevin L. Donihe - A washing machine becomes human and pursues his dream of meeting his favorite soap opera star. **244 pages $11**

BB-082 "Shatnerquake" Jeff Burk - All of the characters ever played by William Shatner are suddenly sucked into our world. Their mission: hunt down and destroy the real William Shatner. **100 pages $10**

BB-083 "The Cannibals of Candyland" Carlton Mellick III - There exists a race of cannibals that are made of candy. They live in an underground world made out of candy. One man has dedicated his life to killing them all. **170 pages $11**

BB-084 "Slub Glub in the Weird World of the Weeping Willows" Andrew Goldfarb - The charming tale of a blue glob named Slub Glub who helps the weeping willows whose tears are flooding the earth. There are also hyenas, ghosts, and a voodoo priest **100 pages $10**

BB-085 "Super Fetus" Adam Pepper - Try to abort this fetus and he'll kick your ass! **104 pages $10**

BB-086 "Fistful of Feet" Jordan Krall - A bizarro tribute to spaghetti westerns, featuring Cthulhu-worshipping Indians, a woman with four feet, a crazed gunman who is obsessed with sucking on candy, Syphilis-ridden mutants, sexually transmitted tattoos, and a house devoted to the freakiest fetishes. **228 pages $12**

BB-087 "Ass Goblins of Auschwitz" Cameron Pierce - It's Monty Python meets Nazi exploitation in a surreal nightmare as can only be imagined by Bizarro author Cameron Pierce. **104 pages $10**

BB-088 "Silent Weapons for Quiet Wars" Cody Goodfellow - "This is high-end psychological surrealist horror meets bottom-feeding low-life crime in a techno-thrilling science fiction world full of Lovecraft and magic..." -John Skipp **212 pages $12**

BB-089 "Warrior Wolf Women of the Wasteland" Carlton Mellick III
Road Warrior Werewolves versus McDonaldland Mutants...post-apocalyptic fiction has never been quite like this. **316 pages $13**

BB-090 "Cursed" Jeremy C Shipp - The story of a group of characters who believe they are cursed and attempt to figure out who cursed them and why. A tale of stylish absurdism and suspenseful horror. **218 pages $15**

BB-091 "Super Giant Monster Time" Jeff Burk - A tribute to choose your own adventures and Godzilla movies. Will you escape the giant monsters that are rampaging the fuck out of your city and shit? Or will you join the mob of alien-controlled punk rockers causing chaos in the streets? What happens next depends on you. **188 pages $12**

BB-092 "Perfect Union" Cody Goodfellow - "Cronenberg's THE FLY on a grand scale: human/insect gene-spliced body horror, where the human hive politics are as shocking as the gore." -John Skipp. **272 pages $13**

BB-093 "Sunset with a Beard" Carlton Mellick III - 14 stories of surreal science fiction. **200 pages $12**

BB-094 "My Fake War" Andersen Prunty - The absurd tale of an unlikely soldier forced to fight a war that, quite possibly, does not exist. It's Rambo meets Waiting for Godot in this subversive satire of American values and the scope of the human imagination. **128 pages $11**

BB-095 "Lost in Cat Brain Land" Cameron Pierce - Sad stories from a surreal world. A fascist mustache, the ghost of Franz Kafka, a desert inside a dead cat. Primordial entities mourn the death of their child. The desperate serve tea to mysterious creatures. A hopeless romantic falls in love with a pterodactyl. And much more. **152 pages $11**

BB-096 "The Kobold Wizard's Dildo of Enlightenment +2" Carlton Mellick III - A Dungeons and Dragons parody about a group of people who learn they are only made up characters in an AD&D campaign and must find a way to resist their nerdy teenaged players and retarded dungeon master in order to survive. 232 **pages $12**

BB-097 "My Heart Said No, but the Camera Crew Said Yes!" Bradley Sands - A collection of short stories that are crammed with the delightfully odd and the scurrilously silly. **140 pages $13**

BB-098 "A Hundred Horrible Sorrows of Ogner Stump" Andrew Goldfarb - Goldfarb's acclaimed comic series. A magical and weird journey into the horrors of everyday life. **164 pages $11**

BB-099 "Pickled Apocalypse of Pancake Island" Cameron Pierce A demented fairy tale about a pickle, a pancake, and the apocalypse. **102 pages $8**

BB-100 "Slag Attack" Andersen Prunty - Slag Attack features four visceral, noir stories about the living, crawling apocalypse. A slag is what survivors are calling the slug-like maggots raining from the sky, burrowing inside people, and hollowing out their flesh and their sanity. **148 pages $11**

BB-101 "Slaughterhouse High" Robert Devereaux - A place where schools are built with secret passageways, rebellious teens get zippers installed in their mouths and genitals, and once a year, on that special night, one couple is slaughtered and the bits of their bodies are kept as souvenirs. **304 pages $13**

BB-102 "The Emerald Burrito of Oz" John Skipp & Marc Levinthal OZ IS REAL! Magic is real! The gate is really in Kansas! And America is finally allowing Earth tourists to visit this weird-ass, mysterious land. But when Gene of Los Angeles heads off for summer vacation in the Emerald City, little does he know that a war is brewing...a war that could destroy both worlds. **280 pages $13**

BB-103 "The Vegan Revolution... with Zombies" David Agranoff When there's no more meat in hell, the vegans will walk the earth. **160 pages $11**

BB-104 "The Flappy Parts" Kevin L Donihe - Poems about bunnies, LSD, and police abuse. You know, things that matter. **132 pages $11**

BB-105 "Sorry I Ruined Your Orgy" Bradley Sands - Bizarro humorist Bradley Sands returns with one of the strangest, most hilarious collections of the year. **130 pages $11**

BB-106 "Mr. Magic Realism" Bruce Taylor - Like Golden Age science fiction comics written by Freud, *Mr. Magic Realism* is a strange, insightful adventure that spans the furthest reaches of the galaxy, exploring the hidden caverns in the hearts and minds of men, women, aliens, and biomechanical cats. **152 pages $11**

BB-107 "Zombies and Shit" Carlton Mellick III - "Battle Royale" meets "Return of the Living Dead." Mellick's bizarro tribute to the zombie genre. **308 pages $13**

BB-108 "The Cannibal's Guide to Ethical Living" Mykle Hansen - Over a five star French meal of fine wine, organic vegetables and human flesh, a lunatic delivers a witty, chilling, disturbingly sane argument in favor of eating the rich.. **184 pages $11**

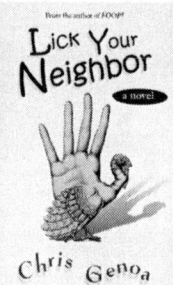

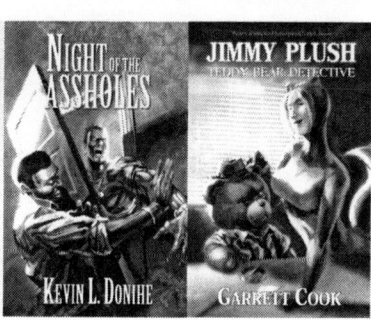

BB-109 "Starfish Girl" Athena Villaverde - In a post-apocalyptic underwater dome society, a girl with a starfish growing from her head and an assassin with sea anenome hair are on the run from a gang of mutant fish men. **160 pages $11**

BB-110 "Lick Your Neighbor" Chris Genoa - Mutant ninjas, a talking whale, kung fu masters, maniacal pilgrims, and an alcoholic clown populate Chris Genoa's surreal, darkly comical and unnerving reimagining of the first Thanksgiving. **303 pages $13**

BB-111 "Night of the Assholes" Kevin L. Donihe - A plague of assholes is infecting the countryside. Normal everyday people are transforming into jerks, snobs, dicks, and douchebags. And they all have only one purpose: to make your life a living hell.. **192 pages $11**

BB-112 "Jimmy Plush, Teddy Bear Detective" Garrett Cook - Hard-boiled cases of a private detective trapped within a teddy bear body. **180 pages $11**